**Two sisters can get into more trouble than one!
Two sisters . . . one sleep-away camp . . . big trouble!**

MICHELLE

Michelle leaned back in her seat and smiled. At that moment, she was glad Camp OutaSight didn't let older sisters counsel their younger sisters' groups. She was happy be be separated from Stephanie. . . .

Yup, Michelle thought. *Camp is going to be much better without my big sister breathing down my neck.*

STEPHANIE

Being assigned to Michelle's group wasn't a bad thing at all. In fact, it was an amazingly *good* thing. . . .

Yes! Stephanie thought. *Having Michelle around will make getting the rest of the bunk in tip-top shape even easier. Not only will that make everyone in the bunk happy, it will make Michelle feel extra special to be my helper. What a perfect plan!*

FULL HOUSE™: SISTERS books

Two on the Town

One Boss Too Many

Available from MINSTREL Books

FULL HOUSE™

SISTERS

One Boss Too Many

Devra Newberger Speregen

A Parachute Book

A
MINSTREL®
BOOK

Published by POCKET BOOKS
New York   London   Toronto   Sydney   Tokyo   Singapore

A MINSTREL PAPERBACK *Original*

A Minstrel Book published by
POCKET BOOKS, a division of Simon & Schuster Inc.
1230 Avenue of the Americas, New York, NY 10020

A PARACHUTE BOOK

Copyright © and ™ 1999 by Warner Bros.

FULL HOUSE, characters, names and all related indicia are trademarks of Warner Bros. © 1999.

ISBN: 0-671-02150-8

First Minstrel Books printing January 1999

10 9 8 7 6 5 4 3 2 1

A MINSTREL BOOK and colophon are registered trademarks of Simon & Schuster Inc.

Cover photo by Schultz Photography

Printed in the U.S.A.

STEPHANIE

Chapter
1

"Are you *sure* you have enough tissues?" Danny Tanner asked as he stuffed a jumbo box of tissues into Stephanie Tanner's overnight bag.

Stephanie groaned. She shook her head so hard that her blond hair whipped her cheeks. "Dad, please," she said. "For the tenth time, I have plenty of tissues. Probably enough for everyone at Camp OutaSight."

"I'm only trying to be helpful, Stephanie," her dad told her. "I want you to be prepared—especially when you're going so far from home."

"It's not that far. And I'll be *fine*," Steph-

1

anie replied. "Spring break is only seven days long." She lowered her voice and glanced quickly around the bus stop. "And I *am* fourteen years old—old enough to be a counselor in training and take care of myself *and* a bunk full of campers!"

How embarrassing! Dad always treats me like I'm four years old, Stephanie thought. *I hope the other CITs didn't hear any of that.*

She had never been part of an offical counselor-in-training program before. It sounded grown-up and important—the perfect way to spend the short spring break from school. If her father didn't ruin it for her before she got on the bus.

Stephanie checked out the other counselors in training. They all seemed to be busy with their parents, too. Nobody was listening to her and her father's conversation. *Good!*

"I wish Michelle was going to be in your bunk," Danny told Stephanie. "Then you could keep an eye out for your little sister."

Soon after Stephanie decided to be a CIT, Michelle announced that *she* wanted to go to camp, too, so her dad signed them both up at Camp OutaSight.

2

"Dad, they never put relatives in the same group," Stephanie told him. "We probably won't even *see* each other all week."

"That's too bad." Danny sighed. "I'm worried that she might get homesick."

"Why would she get homesick? Michelle has been to sleep-away camp before," Stephanie reminded him.

"Are you talking about me?" Nine-year-old Michelle appeared at Stephanie's side, dragging her backpack along the ground. Her strawberry blond hair already looked tangled.

"I just found out that the bus ride to camp is two hours long," Michelle complained. "What are we supposed to do on a dumb bus for two hours?"

"Meet people," Stephanie told her. "Make new friends. That's what camp is all about."

"Stephanie's right," Danny agreed. "I'll bet your new address book will be filled up by the time you get to camp."

Stephanie watched as Michelle gazed around the parking lot. She checked out all the boys and girls who looked around nine or ten.

3

"What if nobody talks to me?" Michelle asked.

"I'll talk to you," Stephanie offered.

"Yeah, but you're my sister," Michelle replied. "I meant what if nobody cool talks to me."

Stephanie put her hands on her hips. "Michelle," she teased. "For your information, I happen to be *very* cool!"

"I *meant* that I want to meet somebody cool in the same age group as me," Michelle explained.

The bus driver poked his head out the bus door. "Five minutes left," he called to everyone. "We have to leave by seven-thirty."

"We should get on the bus," Stephanie said.

Michelle took a deep breath and tried to sling her backpack over her shoulder. "Ugh. How did this get so heavy?" she asked.

"Oh. I was afraid you might not remember your toothbrush," Danny told her. "So I put an extra one in. Plus a few other things."

Michelle unzipped her backpack and looked inside. "I see the extra toothpaste and some dental floss. But what's this?"

She lifted out a plastic bag. It was stuffed with cans of cleaning powder and three new sponges.

"I thought you and Stephanie could use those to scrub down your bunks at camp," Danny said. "You can never be too careful about germs."

"Dad!" Michelle groaned, so did Stephanie. Their father was a total neat freak.

"I don't think we'll have to worry about cleaning our bunks," Stephanie told him. "I'm sure Camp OutaSight is very clean. Besides, we aren't going there to wash floors. We're going to have fun." She gave her father a big hug.

Danny hugged her back, then kissed Michelle. "Okay, then!" he said. "I guess this is good-bye."

Michelle ran over to the bus and climbed up the steps.

"Wait!" Danny called. "Don't you think you two should visit the little girls' room before you get on the bus?"

All over the parking lot people turned to stare at Danny. Some snickered, covering their mouths with their hands.

"Dad!" Stephanie snapped. Her face flushed. Only *her* father would yell across a parking lot about something embarrassing like bathrooms. And to make things worse, he even called it the "little girls' room"!

"Stephanie? Are you Stephanie Tanner?" a voice asked.

She turned and found herself looking at a *very* cute boy, about sixteen or seventeen years old. He wore a white *Camp OutaSight* polo shirt and was holding an official-looking clipboard. Stephanie noticed he had incredibly thick, wavy brown hair and deep brown eyes.

"I'm Cal Mason," he said, smiling. "I've been looking for you!"

Stephanie managed to smile back. She hoped Cal hadn't noticed her red face. Ugh! Leave it to her father to talk about the "little girls' room" in front of a gorgeous guy.

As she took in Cal's face, she realized he looked strangely familiar. *Where do I know him from?* Stephanie wondered.

"Um, why were you looking for me?" she asked.

"I have your counselor-in-training orientation packet." Cal handed her a thick purple-and-white binder and a shiny silver whistle on a long red ribbon.

"I'm head counselor here," Cal added. "Is this your first time working at a camp?"

"Sort of," Stephanie replied. "I was never an official counselor before. But one summer I ran a camp for little kids over at the community pool."

Cal stared at her. "Really? Hey, that must be why you look so familiar. My little sister used to hang out at the community pool. And she used to go to a day camp there! She must have gone to *your* camp!"

Memories flooded Stephanie's mind. Yes. Two summers ago—at the day camp—that's where she'd seen Cal before!

Stephanie's best friends, Darcy and Allie, tried to point Cal out to her more than once. They raved about how cute and nice he was. But Stephanie was too hung up on her summer love, Rick, to notice.

"Sometimes, my mom would ask me to pick up my sister," Cal continued. "She always had such a good time, she hated to leave the pool. That's where I must have seen you." He paused. "Wow! I can't believe you *ran* a whole camp!"

"Yeah. I really love kids. And it *was* a lot of fun," Stephanie told him. "That's why I'm so excited to start a real CIT program."

Cal grinned. "I never heard of a CIT with that much experience before," he said. "Maybe you could give me some tips on running Camp OutaSight."

Stephanie blushed. "I don't know about that. The camp at the pool was really small."

Boy, she thought. *Darcy and Allie were totally right! Cal is cute—and nice. I only just met him, but I think I like him—a lot!*

"Small camp or not," Cal said. "It sounds like I'm lucky to have you around."

"Lucky to have *who* around?" a voice demanded.

A pretty girl about sixteen years old strode up to them. She had the most beautiful long, red hair Stephanie had ever seen. It fell past her shoulders halfway down her back.

"Parker. You have to meet Stephanie," Cal declared. "Stephanie, this is Parker Peterson."

Stephanie smiled. "Hi, Parker. Are you a CIT, too?"

Parker laughed. "I *was* a CIT—two years ago," she said. "Now I'm co–head counselor."

"Parker and I have been friends forever," Cal told Stephanie. He slung an arm around Parker's shoulders. Stephanie noticed a small smile cross Parker's lips.

"Here at Camp OutaSight, Parker's mainly in charge of the CITs," he explained. "You know, making sure everything's going smoothly in all the bunks, helping out in a crisis. That kind of thing." He turned to the older girl. "Parker, you won't believe this. Stephanie ran a whole summer camp."

Parker's eyes widened. "Really?" she asked.

Stephanie nodded. "But nothing as big as this camp," she added.

"Still. That's pretty impressive," Parker told her.

"I'm glad you joined us, Stephanie," Cal said. "Looks like the three of us will be spending a lot of time together. Well, I have to help load the buses. Catch you later!"

Stephanie watched as Cal walked away. She liked the way he was so friendly and outgoing.

"Cal *is* adorable," Parker told her with a grin.

Stephanie blushed. "Yes, he's . . . he seems really nice." It wouldn't be cool to seem too eager about Cal, Stephanie decided.

"He's a lot of fun, too," Parker went on. "*If* you don't get on his bad side."

"Bad side?" Stephanie asked in surprise. She couldn't imagine that Cal had a bad side.

Parker brushed her hair back with her fingers. "Oh, he can be a real pain," she said. "If he thinks you're not doing your job, watch out."

"No way!" Stephanie protested.

"Take it from me," Parker said. "He's one of the toughest head counselors ever. Luckily, I'm his good friend. So he pretty much leaves me alone. If you mess up, don't worry. I'll help you get around him."

Stephanie spotted Cal across the parking lot, goofing around with a couple of little campers. They seemed to be having fun. Could Cal really be the way Parker described?

Stephanie decided she'd figure that out during the week. But one thing was for sure—Parker was one of Cal's best friends. That made her the perfect ally.

If I make a good impression on Parker, Stephanie thought, *then Cal will hear about it and have a good opinion of me. And I totally want Cal to think I'm the best counselor ever. Not just so he thinks I'm doing a good job—but because then maybe he'll like me!*

Parker opened her own loose-leaf binder. "I might as well give you this now," she said. She tore out a sheet of paper and handed it to Stephanie. "This is a list of the jobs the CIT is responsible for in her bunk."

"No problem." Stephanie took the paper and placed it in her notebook to read during the bus ride.

"Just remember, Cal likes hard workers," Parker told her. "Keep things organized. Finish *all* your chores. And keep your bunk extra neat. That will impress him for sure!" She grinned at Stephanie. "Of course, he's impressed with you already."

"You really think so?" Stephanie asked.

"Definitely," Parker told her. "I'm one of his best friends, so I can tell. I never saw him pay so much attention to a CIT before." She paused. "Why don't I save you a seat on the bus? Counselors sit together, up front."

"Sure. I'd like that. Thanks, Parker," Stephanie said.

Parker hurried off to help the other campers. Stephanie grinned. Yes! Parker was totally nice. And the two of them were already getting along.

Stephanie turned and practically skipped back to her dad.

"Remember," Danny told her. "I want you and Michelle to try to help each other out, and—"

"We will, Dad," Stephanie told him. "I've got to get on the bus now, okay?"

"Okay!" He gave Stephanie another hug, then began crossing the parking lot.

"Bye, Stephanie," he called over his shoulder. "Don't forget to use the cleaning supplies!"

Stephanie smiled and watched her dad climb into his car. She felt a little sad. She'd miss the huge family she and Michelle were leaving behind. There was their older sister, D.J., who was in college.

Then there was their dad's best friend,

Joey Gladstone, and her uncle Jesse, who both moved in when Stephanie's mom died to help her dad take care of her and her sisters. They were always fun to hang out with.

Last but not least there was Uncle Jesse's wife, Aunt Becky, and their twin sons, Nicky and Alex. It was fun to see them learn and grow so fast.

Danny pulled away, and Stephanie swallowed the lump that had formed in her throat. She turned toward the bus and quickly felt better. Camp was going to be awesome! She couldn't believe how nice and friendly everyone was.

Especially Cal.

Wow, she thought. *I think I'm about to start the most amazing week of my life!*

MICHELLE

Chapter
2

Michelle gazed across the rows of seats in the bus. A lot of kids were already sitting in the back.

Guess I'll take a place up front, Michelle thought. She started to sink into an empty green seat.

"Hey!" someone called. "The first five rows are saved for counselors and CITs."

Michelle spotted a girl in the tenth row. She had a very round face and a head full of tight golden curls. Some of the curls were pinned back with bright blue glitter barrettes.

"Oh, thanks," Michelle said. She noticed that the seat next to the girl was still empty.

14

She made her way down the aisle and stopped at the tenth row. "Is anybody sitting here?" she asked and pointed at the empty seat.

The curly-haired girl studied Michelle from head to toe. "No," she said. "Nobody's sitting there, but I can't let *you* sit there either."

Michelle blinked at her in surprise. *How rude!* she thought. "Why can't I sit there?" she asked.

The girl leaped up and snatched Michelle's baseball cap off her head. "Because blue baseball caps are not allowed in this seat." She tossed the cap toward the rear of the bus.

"Hey! Give it back!" Michelle exclaimed.

She ran down the aisle and bent to snatch the cap off the floor. But a redheaded boy reached it first. He grabbed it and tossed it to a dark-haired boy, who threw it to a brown-haired girl.

"Come on! Give it back!" Michelle shouted. She leaped at the girl and grabbed the cap away.

She pulled it onto her head and marched back to the curly-haired girl.

"What did you do that for?" she demanded.

The girl laughed. "Sorry. I was just joking around," she explained. "You can sit here if you want. And you can wear your blue cap, too."

Michelle hesitated. "Okay. But I didn't think that was very funny."

"You've never been to Camp OutaSight before, have you?" the girl guessed. "That's just the kind of stuff we do. Everyone jokes around, believe me. And no one gets upset or takes it personally."

"Well, this *is* my first time here," Michelle admitted.

"It's my *third* time. And I know Camp OutaSight inside and out!" The girl grinned. "I'm Mallory. Mallory Lincoln. What's your name?"

"Michelle Tanner," she replied.

"You look about nine or ten," Mallory said. Michelle nodded.

"I'm ten!" Mallory smiled. "That means we could be in the same group. That would be excellent!"

Michelle smiled back. *I guess Mallory isn't*

so bad, after all, she thought. *And, hey, check this out—I'm already making a new friend!*

Mallory poked the redheaded girl sitting directly behind her. "Hey, Courtney! This is Michelle. It's her first time here."

Courtney grinned. "Hi, Michelle!" She pointed at the dark-haired girl beside her. "This is Shari. She's new, too."

"Hi, Shari," Michelle said.

Wow! Mallory knows everybody, she thought. *If I stay friends with her, by the end of camp I'll know everybody, too! And Stephanie said that's what camp's all about—making new friends!*

Just then the bus driver closed the doors, and the bus began to move. A cheer went up. Michelle felt a burst of excitement.

"Uh-oh!" Mallory suddenly whispered. "Don't look now, but one of the CITs is headed this way!"

Michelle peered down the center aisle. The CIT was Stephanie!

Stephanie stopped at Michelle's seat. She stooped down and spoke in her ear.

"Listen, Michelle," Stephanie said. "I'm sitting with Parker Peterson—the co–head counselor. She's in charge of the CITs!"

Stephanie glanced over her shoulder. "Parker wanted to come back here and bawl you out! But I told her I'd take care of it."

Michelle blinked in confusion. "Bawl *me* out? Why?"

Stephanie shot her a stern look. "Because you were throwing your baseball cap all over the bus!" She lowered her voice. "Listen, you don't want to get me in trouble, do you?"

"No. Of course not. It wasn't even my fault," Michelle protested. "See, Mallory was—"

"Just control yourself, okay?" Stephanie interrupted. "I'm trying to make a good impression on Parker. I don't want her to think my sister is the camp troublemaker!"

Before Michelle could say another word, Stephanie hurried back up the aisle.

Michelle's mouth dropped open. What was up with her sister's attitude?

"What was *that* all about?" Mallory asked.

"*That* was my sister!" Michelle told her.

"Your sister is a counselor?" Courtney asked, leaning over the back of Michelle's seat.

Michelle nodded. "A CIT," she explained.

"Why did she seem so upset?" Shari asked.

"She said I was making trouble," Michelle replied.

"What trouble?" Mallory asked.

"That's what I'd like to know!" Michelle insisted. "Stephanie said that someone named Parker saw me jumping around and wanted to come yell at me. But she didn't because Stephanie stopped her."

"Oh! Parker had something to do with this," Mallory said. "That explains it."

"It does?" Michelle asked.

Mallory nodded. "Sure. Parker was a CIT here last year. Everybody hated her! She's the biggest phony-baloney alive."

"Yeah," Courtney added. "Everone knows Parker acts nice. But inside she's totally mean. Especially to her campers."

"The only reason she got to be co–head counselor this year is that she and Cal are friends," Mallory continued. "And she's got Cal convinced she's the best counselor ever!"

Courtney smirked. "That's because Parker really wants to be Cal's *girlfriend*." She said the word in a singsong way. "But Cal's totally not interested."

"Hey," Mallory interrupted. "Remember that girl who liked Cal last year? Parker got totally jealous of her."

"Yeah. She was so jealous, she got the girl kicked out of camp early," Courtney remembered. "She made it look like the girl was a terrible counselor."

"Wow. Parker sounds like bad news," Michelle said. "I bet Stephanie doesn't know any of this. I should warn her."

"Oh, don't worry. She'll find out for herself soon enough," Mallory told her.

"Uh—I guess so," Michelle agreed. "Because Stephanie said she and Parker are working together." She bit her bottom lip.

"Just relax, Michelle. Your sister will be fine," Mallory assured her. "I mean, it's not like she likes Cal or anything. She has nothing to worry about."

Michelle felt a little nervous for her sister. But then she shook her head. Why worry? Stephanie didn't like Cal, as far as she knew. And she certainly could take care of herself.

Besides, right now Michelle had more important things to concentrate on—like making new friends!

Mallory leaned way back and stuck her hands behind her head. She put her feet up on the seat in front of her. "So, who do you think will be our counselor this year?" she asked Courtney.

"Well, we know it won't be Stephanie," Courtney answered. "They never put sisters in the same group."

Michelle leaned back in her own seat and smiled. At that moment she was happy to be separated from Stephanie. It would give her a chance to be herself instead of Stephanie's little sister.

"The first night at camp is a really big night for practical jokes," Mallory explained to Michelle. "Stick with us. You're going to love it!" She leaped up to slap Courtney and Shari a high-five.

"Excellent!" Courtney shouted.

Michelle high-fived Courtney and Shari. Then Mallory held up her hand and Michelle slapped her a high-five, too.

Stephanie would never approve of practical joking, Michelle thought. *Yup, camp is going to be much better without my big sister breathing down my neck.*

21

STEPHANIE

Chapter
3

I can't believe we've been on this bus for almost two hours," Stephanie told Parker.

"Time flies when you're having fun." Parker grinned.

"I guess so!" Parker had talked to Stephanie almost nonstop for the entire trip. She filled her in on Camp OutaSight and gave her lots of advice.

"The camp you ran was small," Parker told Stephanie. "Camp OutaSight is big. There are lots more rules to follow."

"I know. Thanks for all the tips on how to keep my campers in line," Stephanie told her. "I feel much more prepared now."

"Good," Parker told her. "I'm glad to help."

Parker and I are really hitting it off, Stephanie told herself. *I hope she passes the word on to Cal!*

"Hey—we're here!" Parker exclaimed.

Stephanie caught sight of a wooden sign. It announced CAMP OUTASIGHT in tall carved letters.

A cheer went out from the campers. Someone started singing, *"We're here because we're here, because we're here . . ."*

Soon the whole bus joined in.

The campers were on their feet as soon as the bus came to a stop. Parker rose from her seat and slung her bag over her shoulder. "Okay, Stephanie," she said. "Time to get to work!"

Stephanie got up and stretched. "What's first?" she asked.

"First we help Cal get the kids off the bus. Then we lead them to the Meet Site to get their bunk assignments," Parker explained.

"Okay!" Stephanie eagerly followed Parker off the bus.

Outside, the campers unloaded their duffel

bags and backpacks from the storage compartment under the bus.

Tweeeet!!

Parker blew on her whistle. "Listen up, everybody!" she shouted. "Carry all your things to the flagpole. You'll see it on the other side of the bus! Sit down quietly. Then Cal will read out the bunk assignments."

Boy, she really is strict with these kids! Stephanie thought. *But if Cal thinks Parker's a good counselor, I guess I'll have to be a little tougher, too.*

Stephanie rounded up a group of eleven-year-old kids.

Tweeeet!! She blew on her whistle.

"Okay, listen up!" she told them, imitating Parker's voice. "You heard Parker. To the flagpole. March!"

The kids began stomping off, walking single file. Stephanie felt a burst of satisfaction.

All right! she thought. *They really listened to me. So far, so good!*

She turned and caught sight of Michelle. She was struggling with her backpack. "Michelle, do you need some help?" she called.

Michelle brightened. "Yes! That extra stuff Dad packed made this way too heavy."

Stephanie headed toward Michelle.

"Excuse me!" A little girl ran up and tugged on Stephanie's arm. She looked as if she was about to cry.

The girl pointed to Parker. "That lady told me to ask you for help. I can't find my overnight bag. And all my bean-bag babies are in it!"

Stephanie looked at the girl's face. She seemed so sad. "Don't worry." She took the girl's hand. "We'll find your bag, I promise." She turned back to her sister. "Sorry, Michelle. Guess I can't help you now."

Stephanie heard Michelle groan. She hoisted her backpack again and trudged after her own group.

Stephanie glanced at the Meet Site. Most of the kids were already settling in. Cal was trying to quiet them down.

Uh-oh. I'd better hurry, she thought. *Didn't Parker say Cal hated it when counselors were late for meetings?*

Stephanie turned to the little girl. "I'm sure

25

your bag is around someplace. Let's check the bus again."

Stephanie checked every seat in the bus. No bag.

"Oh, wait!" the girl suddenly cried. "I remember! I took it with me when we stopped to use the bathroom. Then I put it into the storage compartment!"

Stephanie found the bus driver and asked him to unlock the storage compartment under the bus. Sure enough, the bag had slid far back into a corner.

"There it is! Oh, thank you!" the girl exclaimed.

"You're welcome," Stephanie said. "But let's get back to the flagpole right away! We don't want to miss anything important."

I hope Cal didn't start assigning bunks yet, she thought.

Stephanie walked quickly to the Meet Site. When she realized what was going on, her heart sank. Cal was already splitting the campers into groups.

Stephanie led the little girl to the youngest group of campers. Then she hurried through the crowd to find Parker.

"Where *were* you?" Parker whispered.

"Helping that little girl find her bag," Stephanie explained.

"You shouldn't have taken so long," Parker said.

Stephanie bit her bottom lip. "Sorry, Parker. It won't happen again, I promise."

"It's no big deal to me." Parker shrugged. "It's just that Cal looked kind of upset that you weren't here on time."

Stephanie groaned. She wanted to kick herself. This was *not* the way to impress Cal!

"Look. Don't sweat it," Parker said. "I managed to smooth it over with him, so don't even give it another thought."

Stephanie breathed a sigh of relief. "Thank you so much!" she said. She glanced around the site. "So where's my group?"

Stephanie's eyes skimmed the crowd of kids waiting for bunk assignments. She spotted Michelle wearing a purple bandanna. She noticed that the girls Michelle sat with on the bus were also wearing purple.

"The next group is the Grape Jammers," Cal announced.

"That explains the purple bandannas,"

Stephanie observed. "It's the color of grape jam."

"Yup. That's the idea," Parker agreed. "I started the whole bandanna thing last summer. It's a fun way to tell the campers apart."

Cal read off a list of six names. ". . . Mallory Lincoln, Courtney Cohen, and Michelle Tanner."

Everyone on the list lifted their bags and walked toward the flagpole.

"Okay," Cal continued. "Grape Jammers, pay attention! The co-head counselor handling your bunk is Parker Peterson, and your bunk's CIT is Stephanie Tanner."

Stephanie blinked in surprise. "Wait a minute!" she exclaimed. "I can't be in charge of them. That's my sister's group!"

Parker stared at her. "You have a sister at camp?"

Stephanie pointed. "Yes. That's Michelle right there . . . in the blue baseball cap."

"Isn't that the troublemaker from the bus?" Parker asked.

Oops! Stephanie flushed. "No! I mean— yes. Well, I mean, she's not usually a trouble- maker," she fumbled.

Parker didn't look convinced. "They *never* put sisters in the same bunk," she said. "Come on. Let's ask Cal about it."

I hope Cal isn't still mad at me for being late for the meeting, Stephanie thought. She followed closely behind Parker.

Cal was handing out yellow bandannas to the Banana Floats group. His face lit up when he saw Stephanie.

"Hey, Stephanie!" He smiled broadly at her. "How do you like your Grape Jammers group?"

"Uh, fine," she answered.

Whoa. Cal didn't seem the least bit angry now. Parker had done a great job smoothing things over! *I was right,* Stephanie thought. *Parker is a good ally.*

"We have a problem," Parker added. "Stephanie's sister Michelle is in her group."

Cal checked his clipboard. "Yikes! Looks like I goofed," he admitted. "We've always put family members into separate groups. Just to make sure counselors don't play favorites in the bunk, or anything like that."

"What are we going to do about it?" Parker asked.

Cal stared at his clipboard. A concerned expression crossed his face.

Stephanie thought for a moment. This might be a good chance to impress Cal with her positive attitude.

"You know, I can treat everyone the same," she said. "I come from a big family, and I have lots of experience with keeping a whole big group of people happy. So you really don't have to switch everyone around. You can count on me not to play favorites with Michelle."

Cal looked relieved. "Wow! That's great! Then I guess we'll leave it the way it is," he said. "If that's okay with you, Parker."

Parker looked slowly from Cal to Stephanie and back to Cal. "Oh, sure," she finally said, and smiled. "If you're happy, I'm happy, Cal."

"Great!" Cal nodded. "Problem solved." He beamed at Stephanie. "Thanks for putting in a major effort here."

"Okay," Parker said. "Better get started, Stephanie. Take your kids to their bunk."

There were four bunkhouses on one side of the field, and four bunks directly across on the other side. The Grape Jammers' bunk sat on the side farthest from the flagpole.

"Get the campers settled in, then start your chores," Parker added.

"Wait." Stephanie shook her head. *"What* chores?"

Parker frowned. "The chores. From the *list* I gave you?" She darted her eyes toward Cal, then stared at Stephanie as if to say, Don't screw up *again.* Cal is watching!

Stephanie sucked in a breath. She had forgotten all about the list of chores. But she couldn't let Cal know that.

"Oh, right. *Those* chores," she said. "I'll get right on them."

"Good, because I have a senior staff meeting with Cal." Parker glanced at her watch. "Our first activity is in one hour. Cal is running the big scavenger hunt." Parker lowered her voice so only Stephanie could hear. "But there might be a surprise inspection. So be sure to supervise your kids extra closely."

"Okay," Stephanie told her. She couldn't wait to get the chores finished. A scavenger hunt sounded like fun.

Stephanie hurried to gather the Grape Jammers together. She could see Michelle talking and laughing with her new friends.

Stephanie smiled. She had just given herself the perfect opportunity to show Cal what she was made of. Cal would think she was the absolute ultimate counselor if she could run the best bunk—despite the fact that her little sister was in it.

Then an amazing thought occurred to her.

Being assigned to Michelle's bunk wasn't a bad thing at all. In fact, it was an amazingly *good* thing! Michelle could be her secret weapon, helping her keep the other Grape Jammers in line!

Yes! Stephanie thought. *Having Michelle around will make getting the bunk in tip-top shape even easier. I'll have more time to do fun stuff with all my campers.*

Not only will that make everyone in the bunk happy and impress Cal, I'm sure it will make Michelle feel extra special to be my helper. What a perfect plan!

MICHELLE

Chapter
4

Michelle spotted her sister heading for the Grape Jammers. She rolled her eyes. *Of all the dumb luck! Just when I was looking forward to a week without Stephanie, she gets assigned to be the CIT for my bunk!*

Tweeeet! Stephanie blew the silver whistle hanging around her neck.

Michelle covered her ears. *Ugh. What an annoying sound.*

"Give me your attention, everyone," Stephanie announced in an official-sounding voice. "We're going to march over to our bunk now. Ready? Go!" *Tweeet!* She blew her whistle—again.

What is up with her? Michelle wondered. *I've never heard Stephanie talk that way before. Ever.*

All the campers reached their bunks and went inside. "I'm going to give out bed assignments," Stephanie told everyone.

She read each name from her list in alphabetical order:

"Courtney Cohen, top bunk of bed one. Shari Franklin, bottom bunk of bed one. Mallory Lincoln, top bunk of bed two. Michelle Tanner, bottom bunk of bed two. Allison Tubman, top bunk of bed three. Jeannie Wilner, bottom bunk of bed three."

"Wait a minute, that isn't fair!" Courtney complained. "I don't like sleeping on a top bunk!"

"Come on, Courtney," Stephanie encouraged. "It's just for a few days."

"But what if I fall off?" Courtney crossed her arms over her chest and pouted.

"You *won't* fall off," Stephanie said.

"How do you know?" Courtney demanded. "Last year I fell off my cousin Rachel's top bunk bed. So there!"

Stephanie took a deep breath, then exhaled. She scanned her list again. "Okay, if you're so freaked out, take Michelle's bed."

"Great!" Courtney swung her backpack onto the bottom bed.

"Hey!" Michelle protested. "I don't want a top bunk either!"

Stephanie pulled her sister aside. "Michelle, please do this favor for me! If Parker thinks I can't even manage a small job like bed assignments . . . that's totally bad news!"

Uh-oh. Parker, Michelle thought. *The counselor that gets people kicked out. Mallory warned me about her. I don't want Stephanie to get in trouble with Parker.*

"Can't you make someone else switch?" Michelle suggested.

"I don't want the other kids to hate me," Stephanie confessed. "Just do this one little favor for me? Please?"

Michelle paused. "Oh, okay," she grumbled.

"Thanks, Michelle." Stephanie squeezed her shoulder.

The girls began to unpack. "Listen up," Stephanie told them. She fished out the list Parker had given her. "We need to do these chores and put this bunk in tip-top shape," she told them. "There may be a surprise inspection later, and we want our bunk to be the neatest!"

Michelle listened as Stephanie carefully explained each chore. Everyone was to start by unpacking her supplies into the cubby next to her bed. The Grape Jammers set right to work.

"Shari!" Stephanie called out. "You're folding your T-shirts all wrong. Fold them horizontally. Then they'll fit better into the cubby!"

Shari made a face. "I only know how to fold them one way," she said.

"Stephanie, you sound like Dad," Michelle complained. "Who cares if our shirts fit exactly into the cubby?"

Stephanie pulled her aside again. "Look, Michelle," she said. "I'm just trying to act like a *real* counselor. I need to impress Parker and Cal. Can't you help me out here?"

Michelle frowned. "I guess I'll help you. But I didn't know *real* counselors had to act so strict. You're not even like this when you baby-sit at home."

There was a knock on the bunk door. A

girl about Stephanie's age walked inside. She spotted Stephanie and smiled. "Hi! I'm Tracy Wells, the CIT for the Apple Dumplings. Parker wants all the CITs to get together for a brief meeting before the scavenger hunt. Want to come with me?"

"Yes, but I can't," Stephanie told her. "We haven't finished our chores yet."

"We could do the rest later," Michelle suggested.

"Parker wouldn't like that," Stephanie said. "But then, she wouldn't want me to miss the meeting either."

She thought for a minute. "I know." She turned to Michelle. "Why don't I put *you* in charge?"

"What? No way." Michelle shook her head. "You're the CIT."

Stephanie lowered her voice. "Look, Michelle, Parker wants the CITs at a meeting. I have to show up. It's no big deal. Just make sure everyone does the chores on this list." She handed her Parker's list. "I'll see you later!"

I don't believe this! Michelle thought. She

stared as Stephanie and Tracy rushed out of the bunk together.

She sighed. Having Stephanie around was putting a serius crimp in her style. If she kept asking Michelle to get her out of tight spots, Michelle was sure to end up with absolutely no friends at all.

Michelle put on her most upbeat expression. "Well, you guys, I guess we're on our own," Michelle told the other campers. "Listen, let's split up the work. Mallory, you and I can straighten the bathroom while the others make all the beds and stuff. It should go quicker that way."

The others agreed to the plan. Michelle and Mallory headed into the bathroom.

Michelle checked Parker's list. "Okay, we have to make sure the shelves are clean in each shower stall," Michelle said. "And then we set a fresh bar of soap on each shelf."

They got down to work.

"Is your sister going to put you in charge all week?" Mallory asked.

"She better not!" Michelle exclaimed. "I didn't come here to be a dumb counselor."

Michelle reached into a shower stall to set down a bar of soap.

"Hmm. Think it looks like rain today, Michelle?" Mallory asked.

"Rain? How should I know?" Michelle began. "First of all, we're inside. And—"

The shower squeaked on. Ice-cold water poured down onto Michelle's head.

"*Hey . . . aaaaghhhh! Aaaghhh!*" Michelle screamed. She held her hands up to block the stream of water, but it was too strong. Icy water tingled on her scalp. It matted her clothes to her body.

"Stop! Stop!" she yelled. She backed out of the stall and felt her feet sliding out from under her. Michelle flailed her arms. She tried to regain her balance.

"Whoa! Whooooa!" she cried.

She fell to the tile floor with a thud. *Wham!* Right on the seat of her pants.

Michelle shook her head. Sprays of water shot out from her soaking-wet hair. A huge puddle spread out around her feet.

Well, she thought. *I'm not hurt.* She reached down and tried to wring out her soaking-wet T-shirt. *Just embarrassed.*

"What was that about?" she demanded, turning to face Mallory.

Mallory burst out laughing. "Hey, Michelle—swimming isn't until *after* lunch!"

"You . . . you did that on *purpose?*" Michelle stared at her new friend in disbelief. The other girls ran in to see what all the fuss was about.

"Here's a tip, Michelle," Mallory said. "Never turn your back on anyone in the shower room!"

Courtney started laughing. "You should see your face!" she cried. Jeannie, Shari, and Allison started laughing, too.

"This isn't funny! I feel disgusting," Michelle said. She shoved strands of wet hair behind her ears.

"Oh, come on, Michelle. You have to admit I got you good. And it *was* pretty funny!" Mallory handed her a big, dry towel.

Michelle snatched the towel and dried off her face. "Funny?" Michelle declared. "I'll show you what's funny!" She jumped up and took an angry step toward Mallory. Her sneakers made a loud sloshing noise.

Everyone broke into fresh fits of laughter.

Michelle bit her lip. She didn't want to seem like a spoilsport. She wanted to make friends, didn't she?

She smiled, then burst out laughing, too. "Okay. It *is* kind of funny," she told everyone.

Mallory grinned. "I'm sorry you got upset, Michelle," she said. "It was just a practical joke. Don't be mad."

"I'm not mad anymore," Michelle fibbed. She dried her hair. "Just wet!"

"You should change before the scavenger hunt," Shari told her.

Everyone went into the main room again. Michelle peeled off her wet clothes and pulled on a clean, dry outfit.

"Mallory is the queen of practical jokes," Courtney told her. "Last year, there was this girl who wouldn't share snacks with anyone. One day, she got a huge box of fancy cookies. Mallory dumped out all the cookies— and put frogs in the box instead!"

"You should have seen *her* face when she reached in for a treat!" Mallory chuckled.

"And what about what you did to June,

our counselor two years ago?" Courtney
went on.

"We couldn't stand June," Mallory explained. "One night, she went out to party
with the other counselors. So we took her
bed and her cubby—and moved them outside, onto the playing field!"

None of this seems very nice, Michelle
thought. *But if everyone else thinks it's
funny . . .*

"No way!" Michelle said with a laugh.

"Well, she deserved it," Mallory said. "She
was really mean."

"Even meaner than Stephanie?" Shari
asked.

"Definitely," Mallory replied.

Michelle sucked in a breath. Did her bunk
mates really think her sister was mean?
Stephanie would be crushed if she knew that.

Courtney giggled. "Hey! Why don't we
pull that same prank on Stephanie?"

Mallory's eyes lit up. "That's an excellent
idea!"

"I don't know, guys," Michelle said. "She
is my sister."

Courtney frowned. "But she put you in charge and went off to have fun."

"Yeah, that's pretty mean," Allison agreed.

"But it's only her first day here," Michelle explained. "She's just trying to be a good counselor. Can't we give her another chance?"

Mallory shrugged. "Well, I guess that's okay with me. It *is* only our first day."

The others agreed.

Good, Michelle thought. *I don't want my new friends to think my sister is a total loser!*

"Thanks, you guys," Michelle said. She glanced at the clock on the cabin wall. "Hey, it's almost time for the scavenger hunt to start."

"We should get over there," Shari said.

"But what about the rest of our chores?" Allison asked. She shuddered as she glanced at the messy bunk.

"I know!" Michelle grabbed a blanket from her cubby and draped it over her bed. It covered all her unpacked clothes. "There! Bed's made!" she announced.

She opened her backpack and dumped the rest of her things into her cubby. Half of her stuff landed on the floor, so she kicked them under the bed.

"And I'm finished unpacking!" she announced.

Mallory laughed, then made her bed and dumped out her bag, too. "So am I!" she cried.

They all shoved their things into their cubbies and under their beds.

"Looks good to me," Michelle declared. "Okay, Grape Jammers! Let's hit the scavenger hunt!"

Michelle linked arms with Mallory and Courtney. Soon all of the girls were walking arm in arm across the field.

Now this *is* what *I* call *fun*, Michelle thought. *Stephanie will never know we took a few shortcuts!*

STEPHANIE

Chapter
5

Stephanie was glad Tracy had told her about the CIT meeting. Parker was already sitting cross-legged on the field by the flagpole as she and Tracy approached.

"Hey, Stephanie," she called. "Hi, Tracy, come join us."

She moved over to make room, and Stephanie and Tracy sat down. Stephanie sat right next to Parker.

"Everyone was just complaining about their campers," she joked. "Sounds like a pretty wild mob."

Just then Cal approached the group. "Hey, everybody!" He glanced at Parker. "Having a CIT meeting already?" he asked.

"Sure, Cal," Parker responded. "I want to make sure our CITs know exactly what they're doing."

"Great!" Cal said. "Mind if I join you?"

Parker moved to her right, shoving Stephanie down a few feet. "Sit right here." Parker patted the ground beside her. Stephanie frowned. She had hoped Cal would choose to sit next to her.

"Thanks, but I think I'll sit among the common people," Cal joked. He moved around Parker and took a seat between Tracy and Stephanie.

Stephanie's heart gave a flutter. Cal was sitting so close that their knees were nearly touching.

Wow. Stephanie thought. *Cal is so amazingly cute!* She took in his long, tan legs and his bright smile.

Stephanie glanced up at Parker. What was that weird expression on her face? Oh, well, Stephanie reasoned. Parker was probably just hoping her best friend would sit next to her.

"So, tell me," Parker began. "Anyone's group causing them trouble?"

"Not my group," Stephanie volunteered.

"They're a great bunch. In fact, I left them hard at work, cleaning and straightening up the bunk."

Cal frowned. "Really?" He paused. "Do you think it was best to put your campers right to work, Stephanie? Maybe you should have given them a chance to break the ice— get to know one another first."

Stephanie swallowed. She didn't know what to say. Hadn't Parker told her Cal would like it if she kept an orderly bunk? She had to think of something—quick!

"Uh—it's my experience that working to-gether to accomplish a task brings people to-gether," Stephanie said. "In its own way, doing chores *will* help the campers break the ice."

Cal beamed at her. "Wow. Your previous camp experience really shows, Stephanie. I never would have thought of that. Good job."

Stephanie felt herself blush. She never would have thought to put the girls in her bunk right to work either.

"Parker helped," she admitted. "She gave

me a list of things to do. It really helped get us organized."

"Really?" Cal glanced at Parker. "That's interesting."

"Listen, Stephanie, we were going to have bunk inspections," Parker put in quickly. "Mind if we inspect your bunk first?"

Stephanie thought of Michelle back at the bunk, directing the girls to straighten everything up. "Be my guest. My bunk will be in tip-top shape," she said.

Stephanie felt a burst of pride. Thanks to her enthusiasm—and Parker's list—she was really going to make a great impression on Cal.

She and Parker really made a great team.

Cal then spoke for about ten minutes. He tried to make the CITs feel welcome, but he also told them he expected them to keep their groups in good order. "That way, everyone can have fun," he explained.

Parker passed him some sheets of paper. "Thanks, Parker," Cal told her. He turned to the group. "The campers will be here soon. So I'll explain how our first event, the scavenger hunt, works. Then you can take over," he said.

"Each bunk is a team. You have to find as many of the objects on your list as you can," he explained. "You can't change the objects. The first group to bring back the most objects wins the hunt."

"How long does it usually take?" Tracy asked.

"Sometimes all day." Cal chuckled. "But we'll stop the hunt at lunchtime, no matter what. Whoever finds the most objects by then wins. Just remember, nobody really expects you to find all ten things."

Soon the campers began crossing the field.

Stephanie spotted the Grape Jammers headed her way. "Michelle! Over here," Stephanie called. She hurried to meet them.

"Here's our list for the scavenger hunt." Stephanie handed Michelle the list. Then she explained how the hunt worked.

She handed Mallory a pad and a pencil. "Michelle can read the objects on the list," she said. "Mallory can write down where we might find each thing."

"All right. Let the fun begin!" Mallory cheered.

"The first object is a Q-Tip," Michelle read.

"I have one back at the bunk!" Courtney exclaimed.

"Next is a black bandanna," Michelle said.

Stephanie and the girls glanced around the field. All the campers wore colored bandannas. But none of them wore black.

"That's a tough one. Let's come back to it later," Stephanie suggested. "Michelle, read the next objects."

"A CIT's paperback book," Michelle said.

All the girls looked at Stephanie.

Stephanie smiled. "No problem. I'm in the middle of a great mystery. It's back at the bunk!"

"Good," Mallory said, writing it down.

"A strand of hair from a senior counselor." Michelle frowned.

"You've got to be kidding!" Shari exclaimed.

"Maybe Parker will give us some of her hair," Mallory joked. "She's got enough of it."

Everyone laughed.

"Why don't we just check her hairbrush?" Stephanie suggested.

The girls agreed that was the best idea. Mallory wrote it down.

"A Band-Aid, a live insect, and a stopwatch," Michelle continued.

"The nurse at the infirmary should have a Band-Aid," Stephanie told them.

"And I can find an insect," Allison said. "I'll catch one in a cup."

"What about the stopwatch?" Michelle asked.

"I bet there's one in the shed where they keep the sports equipment," Stephanie said.

Mallory scribbled furiously. "Check sports shed," she said as she wrote.

"Only three things left," Michelle told them. "An original poem that rhymes, a funky dance step, and a pair of underwear!"

All the girls cracked up.

"I'm not giving you *my* underwear," Allison called out. "Not in a coed camp. I don't want any boy campers staring at them."

"I have a pair of boxer shorts that I usually sleep in," Shari said. "Do they count as underwear?"

Stephanie nodded. "Definitely! Now, what about the poem? Is anybody a decent writer?"

"My English teacher says I'm pretty good," Courtney said.

"Can you write us a poem?" Stephanie asked her. "Nothing fancy. Just four lines or so. As long as it rhymes."

"Sure," Courtney nodded.

"Great!" Stephanie exclaimed. "Just one more thing left."

"A funky dance step," Michelle read.

Jeannie's face lit up. "I can do the macarena!" she shouted.

"We have nine out of ten things." Stephanie grinned. "We could really win this thing!"

Everyone cheered.

Yes, Stephanie thought. *Now we have some team spirit. This is fun!*

"Okay," Stephanie said. "I think the best plan is to split up in groups of two and find different things. Let's meet here in a half hour with all the objects we've collected."

"Michelle, why don't you and Mallory

come with me to find the stuff in our bunk?"
she suggested.

The girls split up. Stephanie, Michelle, and
Mallory raced to the bunk.

Stephanie flew up the steps and pushed
open the door. She burst inside, and gasped
in horror. "Wh-what happened in here?"
she cried.

"Nothing. What's the problem?" Michelle
asked.

Stephanie blinked in shock as she gazed
around at the bunk. "You call this *nothing*?"
she asked. "This place is a pigsty! It's a complete disaster! Michelle, I thought you said
you guys did all the chores!"

"We did," Michelle told her. "We unpacked everything and made the beds."

"But your clothes are just shoved into your
cubbies, there are things sticking out from
under every bed, and the beds are lumpy
disasters!"

Stephanie thought, *What if Cal had inspected
the bunks before I had a chance to see them? It
would have been horrible!*

And, she realized. *It would have been Mi-*

chelle's fault! Stephanie nearly shook with anger.

"Michelle, I can't believe you did this to me! How could you let everyone leave the bunk like this?"

"We had to be fast," Mallory pointed out. "The list of chores was too long, and it was time to go to the scavenger hunt."

"We didn't want to miss it," Michelle added.

A loud rap sounded on the bunk door. A second later it flew open and Parker walked in with Cal.

Stephanie closed her eyes. *Tell me this isn't happening!* She wanted to run and hide under her bed. *How am I going to explain this? Cal's going to think I'm a total loser!*

She held her breath as Cal stood, gaping at the mess. "I thought you said your bunk was clean," he said to Stephanie.

Behind him, Parker bit her lip, as if to say, Oh, boy, this isn't going to be pretty.

Stephanie gulped. "Wait! I can explain," she began.

Cal shook his head and wrote something down on his clipboard. "You know, when

Parker was CIT of this bunk, it was the best at camp."

Stephanie felt horrible. Cal *did* think she was a loser. Plus, Cal was her boss! If he didn't think she was doing a good job, he could fire her!

"Don't worry, Cal," Parker said. "We'll have this place spotless in a flash. Right, Stephanie?"

"Absolutely," Stephanie promised.

Cal left the bunk. Stephanie let out a small groan and slumped down on one of the bunks.

"Parker, I'm so sorry," Stephanie apologized.

"I'll smooth things over with Cal," Parker told her. "Just make sure you get this place cleaned up before lunch. Cal's sure to come back to inspect again." Parker hurried to follow Cal out.

Stephanie whirled to face Michelle. "I am totally humiliated!" she exploded. "You're really lucky Parker was so nice about it. Did you see Cal's face? He was furious!"

Nobody spoke.

"Right now I'm going to find the others,"

Stpehanie told them. "And nobody is leaving this bunk until it's spotless."

"But what about the hunt?" Michelle asked.

"I don't care!" Stephanie snapped. "Don't you realize stuff like this can get me thrown out of the CIT program?"

She grabbed the pen and pencil from Mallory and scribbled something down. She thrust it at Michelle.

"What's this?" Michelle asked.

"A new list of chores," Stephanie declared. "You're in charge again, Michelle. And this time you're going to get this right. None of you leave here until every last chore is finished! Got that?"

Stephanie stomped through the doorway and down the bunk porch steps.

I can't believe this! So much for team spirit! she thought. *No one knows I like Cal, but I thought at least my own sister would want to keep me from getting into trouble with him!*

The only person who seems to be looking out for me is Parker. So from now on, I'm following her example. And listening only to her advice!

MICHELLE

Chapter
6

I can't believe we spent more than an hour mopping, scrubbing, and straightening the whole bunk," Michelle complained.

"Me neither. I don't even have these chores at home," Mallory added.

"I'm not cleaning another thing at camp," Courtney protested. "I'll quit first."

"Me, too," Jeannie chimed in.

"Me three," Allison agreed. She turned to Michelle. "I think your sister must be the meanest CIT that ever lived."

"Yeah!" Mallory nodded. "Now we *have* to move Stephanie's things outside. She deserves it!"

Mallory, Allison, Jeannie, and Courtney went on complaining about Stephanie in loud voices, and Michelle didn't blame them. Stephanie *was* mean. She actually made them scrub the whole bunkhouse before she let them go to lunch.

Even worse, they were too late to finish the scavenger hunt.

Michelle stared over her shoulder at the CIT table. Stephanie sat happily eating lunch with her new friend, Tracy.

She acts like she doesn't care about us at all, Michelle thought. *All she cares about is impressing her bosses—stupid Parker and Cal. Maybe we* should *play a mean trick on her!*

"I just wish we could think of something *worse* than putting her stuff outside," Mallory said. "Maybe we could—"

"Shhh!" Courtney warned. "She's coming over here!"

Michelle and the others grabbed their sandwiches and pretended to be busy eating.

"Hey, guys," Stephanie said. She stood awkwardly behind Michelle. "Listen, I'm sorry I lost my temper before. But I was afraid Cal would totally freak out at how our bunk looked."

"I like Cal— Uh, I mean, I'd like to make a good impression on him. He is my boss and everything. You guys *do* understand that—right?" Stephanie asked.

Nobody looked up or said a word.

"And I'm sorry you missed the scavenger hunt, too," she went on. "The Apple Dumplings finished their list in twenty minutes. We would have lost anyway."

"*We?*" Mallory raised an eyebrow. "*We* were too busy cleaning the bunk to worry about savenger hunts."

"Yeah, and you just stormed out. You didn't even help us!" Courtney added.

Michelle glanced up. Stephanie looked hurt. "I'm trying to apologize here," she told them.

Again, nobody said anything. Michelle twisted her napkin into a knot. Stephanie really was sorry, she could tell. And the Grape Jammers had made her look bad in front of her boss. All Michelle wanted to do was accept Stephanie's apology. But she didn't want to look totally uncool in front of the whole bunk. If she forgave Stephanie now, she'd look like a traitor.

Everyone remained silent.

"Well, anyway, you have something fun to do tomorrow," Stephanie said. She glanced at her clipboard and forced a big, phony smile. "You get to make banners for the big carnival at the end of the week! Doesn't that sound like fun?"

"No," Mallory mumbled.

Michelle winced. Mallory didn't need to say that.

Stephanie ignored her. "It will be a great time. We'll meet at the arts and crafts pavilion at noon." She turned and walked back to her table.

"Yuck! Who wants to make stupid banners?" Courtney grumbled as soon as Stephanie was gone.

"Not me." Mallory made a disgusted face. "Too bad we're stuck with Miss Mean for a CIT."

Michelle just glanced from one bunk mate to the other. She didn't know what to say or do. She had been angry at Stephanie, too, but the others were being awfully rude to her.

And hearing them call her sister *mean* made her really uncomfortable. Stephanie wasn't mean *all* the time.

"Maybe it won't be so bad," Michelle finally said.

Mallory and Courtney exchanged annoyed looks.

Uh-oh, Michelle thought.

"Listen," Mallory started, "If you'd rather hang out with your CIT sister than us—"

"No. No, that's not what I meant," Michelle interrupted.

She took a deep breath. "I meant, we can still have fun being together—no matter what Stephanie does. Right?"

"I guess," Shari said.

Mallory frowned. "Michelle's right," she told the group.

"Right!" Michelle grinned at her. She felt much better.

"You know, painting these banners *is* kind of fun," Mallory admitted.

She, Michelle, Courtney, Shari, Allison, and Jeannie were sprawled in the grass outside the arts and crafts pavilion the next afternoon.

Michelle dipped her brush into the neon-red paint again. The letters leaped out: SPRING CARNIVAL!!

She added an outline of glitter glue around each letter and stepped back to eye the effect. It looked great!

"Your banner is terrific, Michelle!" Stephanie's voice rang out.

Michelle spun around. Stephanie stood behind them, holding extra containers of paint.

"Thanks," Michelle said. She smiled at her sister.

Stephanie eyed the other five banners. They were spread over the porch as the girls worked.

"Is that all you've gotten done?" Stephanie frowned.

"Yes," Michelle told her, feeling annoyed. She saw the others exchange annoyed glances, too.

"Cal's coming over to see these soon," Stephanie pointed out. "I hope they're done by then."

If Michelle could have done it without anyone seeing her, she would have stepped on Stephanie's toe to keep her quiet. The more Stephanie talked like that, the more Michelle's bunk mates were going to dislike her. Didn't she see that?

Stephanie squinted at Mallory's banner. "Mallory, what is that scribble in the corner?"

"It's a pie," Mallory explained. "The red parts are cherries."

"I don't mean to hurt your feelings, Mallory, but it just looks messy." Stephanie picked up Mallory's paintbrush and painted on the pie. "There . . . now it looks like a pie." Stephanie smiled. "Cal will just love it!"

Mallory's mouth dropped open. She stared at Stephanie in shock. "I can't believe you painted over my banner!" she exclaimed.

Michelle had to admit that she couldn't believe her sister had done that either. She glanced over Stephanie's shoulder and spotted Cal climbing up the steps to the pavilion.

"Hey, nice banners!" Cal declared. "I love the glitter glue. Good work, guys." Cal gave Stephanie's arm a little squeeze. "Good job, Stephanie."

"Thanks," Stephanie said, grinning at him.

Michelle's mouth dropped open. *Uh-oh. Wait a minute. What's going on here?*

She stared harder at her sister's expression. *I recognize that goofy grin*, Michelle thought. *It's the Stephanie's-going-loopy-in-love look. Whoa! I can't believe it—Stephanie likes Cal!*

"Listen, Stephanie," Cal went on. "I need to discuss carnival ideas with all the CITs. When you're done with the banners, put them into the pavilion to dry. Then meet us at the flagpole for a short meeting, okay?"

"Sure." Stephanie stared after Cal as he bounded away.

Michelle chuckled to herself. No wonder her sister had been acting so crazy about impressing Cal. Not only was he her boss, she wanted him to like her as a girlfriend.

Michelle stooped to finish her poster. "Hey, Grape Jammers!" a voice greeted them. Michelle glanced up. Uh-oh! Parker! She'd forgotten about her!

Michelle swallowed hard. Wait a second. Didn't Mallory say Parker got a counselor who liked Cal kicked out of camp?

A counselor who liked Cal, Michelle thought.

A counselor like Stephanie. I have to let her know what Parker is really like!

"Your banners look great," Parker added. "Stephanie, when you finish these, carry them down to the sports hut, okay?"

"Oh, but Cal said to put them—" Stephanie began.

Parker frowned. "Listen," she told Stephanie. "Cal didn't know I need all the banners at the sports hut as soon as possible." She glanced at her watch. "I'd help you carry them, but I'm late. Catch you later!"

"Okay, guys," Stephanie said. "You heard Parker. Let's get these banners down to the sports hut."

"But," Michelle tried to protest. Stephanie didn't know what Parker was up to, but she could be telling Stephanie to take the banners to the wrong place on purpose!

"We're—we're not done yet!" She tried to stall for time.

"Michelle." A stern look crossed Stephanie's face. "I can't screw this up! Not after what happened with the bunk yesterday afternoon."

"But—" Michelle tried again.

"Just do it!" Stephanie yelled.

Everyone stared at Stephanie. Including Michelle. How could her sister yell at her that way, especially since she was only trying to help her out?

"It's going to be hard carrying wet banners all the way down the hill," Michelle pointed out. "It might go faster if you and Parker helped us."

Stephanie checked her watch. "Cal wants me to be at a CIT meeting in five minutes. I can't help you. Just get those banners down the hill. I have to get to that meeting. I'll see you back at the bunk."

She ran off without a backward glance.

"She is so incredibly mean!" Mallory stomped her foot.

Courtney, Shari, Jeannie, and Allison nodded in agreement.

"Now, wait, she's not always . . ." Michelle began to defend her sister.

Wait! What am I doing? she wondered. *Stephanie is mean. In fact, she's totally obnoxious! If Parker is trying to sabotage her, she deserves it. She has no real reason to act badly toward us.*

"What is it, Michelle?" Mallory asked. "Are you going to tell us she didn't mean it?"

"Not this time," Michelle said. "I've had it with her."

Mallory and the others cheered.

"I'm not going to try to help her anymore," Michelle went on. "As far as I'm concerned, Stephanie's on her own."

STEPHANIE

Chapter
7

W hat kind of booths are we running this year?" Stephanie asked. She sat next to Cal. The other CITs were grouped in a circle around them.

"Every bunk votes on its own booth," Cal replied. "The campers have to like the booth. After all, this carnival is for them. First they'll build the booths, then they'll get to enjoy them! Last year there were games, and some rides, too."

"Last year's carnival was great!" Tracy told Stephanie.

"I have an idea," a CIT named Carla chimed in. "I was at a school carnival once where they built a whole miniature golf course. They used old dolls and toys and stuff. It was the most popular game at the whole carnival."

"That's a great idea." Stephanie could picture it already.

A CIT named Gabe shook his head. "At my school fairs, the most popular thing is always the dunking booth."

"Definitely popular," Cal agreed.

"A dunking booth?" Stephanie asked. "You mean, where you throw a ball and if it hits the target a person gets dunked in a tank of water?"

"Right," Gabe answered.

"These ideas sound great," Stephanie put in. "But where do we get the supplies to build all these booths?"

"That's all taken care of," Cal told her. "You can check out the storage room in the sports hut after the meeting. Most of the basics are there. Once your campers pick the kind of booth they want, make a list of anything additional you might need, and bring it to me."

"Okay." Stephanie smiled. "This really sounds like fun."

"It is," Cal agreed. "And the campers really have to work hard to pull it together by the end of the week." He glanced at his watch. "Let's make a list of more suggestions for booths and activities. I'll collect the suggestions before the bonfire tomorrow night. Then the entire camp can vote on them."

Stephanie quickly finished her list of suggestions. She wanted to get back to the Grape Jammers as soon as possible. Things had been going so badly with the group that she wanted to bring them the news about the bonfire. That was sure to put them in a better mood.

Right before dinner, when Stephanie gave them the news, she got just the reaction she expected. As angry as they had been with her, the Grape Jammers were still excited about the bonfire. Stephanie watched as they buzzed about what to wear to the big event.

Actually, Stephanie was totally psyched, too. She was planning to stake out a seat right next to Cal!

"Cool!" the girls all chimed.

Parker marched up to the group. "Stephanie, did you think that was *funny?*" she snapped. Everyone in the Grape Jammers stopped talking.

"Parker, what are you talking about?" Stephanie asked as Parker led her away to speak privately with her.

"I'm talking about the banners!" Parker replied. "I thought I *told* you to bring them down to the sports hut to dry!"

"You *did* tell me," Stephanie replied. What was Parker talking about?

Angry red circles popped out in Parker's cheeks. "Stephanie, I just walked past the arts and crafts pavilion, and your banners were lying all over the ground! I had to round up another bunk to help carry the banners to the sports hut."

Stephanie gulped. "Are you kidding?"

"Do I look like I'm kidding?" Parker asked.

Stephanie couldn't believe it. She felt her face turn red with anger. Why hadn't Michelle made sure everyone did the right thing? "I'm really sorry, Parker. I told my group to take the banners to the hut."

"I'm sure they would have if you had supervised them," Parker pointed out.

"But Cal needed me to attend the CIT meeting," Stephanie answered, feeling desperate. "I couldn't be in two places at once. Let me talk to my group and find out what happened."

Parker frowned. "Look, I like you, Stephanie. But this is getting to be a real problem. If you can't keep your campers in line, I don't think I'll be able to hide it from Cal much longer."

Stephanie felt a lump form in her throat. "It won't happen again. I promise."

Parker sighed. "It's just a shame. Because I can tell Cal really likes you. But this kind of slip up makes him really angry!"

Stephanie felt even worse. "Should I explain what happened to him?"

Parker shook her head. "No. Just talk to your campers. I'll smooth things over with Cal—again. But then I have another job for you."

"Another job?" Stephanie echoed.

"Tomorrow I need you to head over to unload some extra firewood from the wood-

shed and then bring it to the bonfire," she
said.

"Okay," Stephanie said. "But, uh, how
much firewood should I unload?" she asked.

"Whatever's in the shack," Parker told her.
"Now go give your campers a stern talking-
to. They could use it."

Stephanie turned and saw Michelle and
her friends laughing and whispering. Did
they think this was funny? Stephanie had almost lost her job because of their carelessness!

How could they be so selfish and imma
ture, when Stephanie was doing her best to
follow orders?

"Can someone please tell me what's going
on?" Stephanie demanded.

The girls gazed up at her, looking wide-
eyed and innocent.

"What are you talking about?" Michelle
asked.

"I'm talking about the banners," Stephanie
replied. "And why Parker found them lying
all over the ground instead of in the sports
hut."

Michelle shrugged.

Stephanie felt a burst of anger. "Michelle!

You deliberately left the banners outside, didn't you? I want to know why and—"

"Is everything all right here, Stephanie?"

Stephanie spun around. Cal!

"Parker said I could find you here. You seem upset. Is something wrong?" Cal seemed really concerned.

This is so humiliating! Stephanie felt her cheeks turn bright red. She took a deep breath. *Cal probably thinks I'm the worst counselor ever, yelling at my campers!*

"Um, no, it's nothing, really," she told him. "We just had a little misunderstanding." She tried to smile.

"Anything I can help with?" Cal asked.

"No, really," she assured him. "It was my fault, anyway. I thought I asked the girls to bring their banners down to the sports hut to dry."

"Why would you bring them to the sports hut? I thought I asked you to put them in the pavilion?" Cal said.

Stephanie frowned. "You did, but Parker wanted them in the sports hut."

"Oh, just a little confusion, I guess. It's really no big deal," Cal said. Then he continued in a low voice. "But, listen, I don't think yelling at your campers is appropriate, Stephanie. I hope I don't see you doing this kind of thing again."

Stephanie felt tears of frustratin well up in her eyes. For some reason, it felt as if she couldn't do anything right!

Cal must think I'm a total idiot. She felt more miserable than ever.

"Okay! Grape Jammers, I want you all to get psyched for our bonfire tomorrow night! I'll see you all later," Cal cheered. "And don't forget—we're going to vote on the booths you'll all have at your carnival at the bonfire, so be sure to come up with some super ideas!"

Cal turned to Stephanie. "Hey, did Parker talk to you about the firewood yet?"

"Yes," Stephanie said. "It's all arranged."

"Good!" he said. "It shouldn't take so long with two people transporting the wood. I'd better run. See you!"

Stephanie didn't hear anything Cal said after "two people transporting."

Is Cal helping me with the firewood? she wondered. Parker hadn't mentioned *that!*

Stephanie stared after Cal as he crossed the field.

She couldn't believe it. *Parker thinks I totally messed up with the banners, but she still found time to get me and Cal together.*

Michelle giggled, interrupting Stephanie's thoughts. Stephanie turned back to the campers. Instantly the giggling stopped.

Stephanie stared at Michelle. She had a mischievous look on her face. Stephanie knitted her eyebrows together.

That's Michelle's I'm-up-to-something look, she realized. But what could she be up to?

MICHELLE

Chapter 8

"All right! I love having pizza for dinner."

At the mess hall the following night, Michelle eagerly reached out to grab a steaming slice of pizza. "Pepperoni—my favorite." She slid the slice off the serving tray onto her plate. Her friends also helped themselves.

She glanced around the mess hall. All the campers, counselors, and CITs were gathered in the huge room—all talking and eating at once. The noise was deafening. And totally fun!

"Pizza or not—don't forget, we still have the world's worst counselor," Mallory pointed out.

"Don't remind me," Michelle grumbled,

still mad at her sister. She saw Stephanie heading their way. "Here she comes now!"

Stephanie reached their table and made Michelle shove over to make room for her on the bench.

"You guys look like you're having a great time," Stephanie told them.

"No thanks to you," Jeannie mumbled.

Michelle snickered. She saw Stephanie open her mouth to say something back to Jeannie, but she stopped herself and faced Michelle instead.

"Listen, Michelle, I need you to help me," Stephanie began. "I just volunteered our group to clean up the mess hall tonight. Parker said it was a good idea. And that we'd be setting a good example for the others."

"In charge of cleanup? What does that mean?" Michelle asked.

"It means I want you and the others to clear all the tables in the mess hall," Stephanie replied.

Michelle's mouth dropped open. "Clear all of them? You volunteered us to clear all the tables? Why? We all clear our own tables."

"It's a good way for us to show Parker

what a terrific group we are," Stephanie explained.

"We *are* terrific," Michelle muttered under her breath. "I can't believe you're making us clear everyone's trash to prove it!"

Michelle glanced over at the long row of huge blue plastic bins. Each bin was labeled with a sign for recycling glass, plastic, or paper. Next to the bins was a table where the plastic serving trays were stacked.

"I really don't see why our bunk has to work for the whole camp," Michelle grumbled.

Stephanie bent over and lowered her voice. She looked really annoyed. "Come on, Michelle. I'm trying really hard to please everyone here. So stop whining about everything." Stephanie glanced up. "Uh-oh. Here comes Parker."

Stephanie blew on her silver whistle. *Tweeeet!*

Michelle cringed. "Will you stop blowing that thing?" she said between clenched teeth.

Stephanie ignored her. "Okay, everyone!" she called in her bossiest voice, imitating Parker. "Pay attention to Michelle! She'll lead in clearing all the tables and recycling the trash!"

Stephanie dropped a plastic serving tray onto Michelle's lap.

"But I'm not done eating," Michelle protested.

"Clean up anyway," Stephanie told her. She whirled around to smile at Parker. As she turned, she knocked into Michelle's pizza plate. It tumbled off the table.

"Oh, no!" Michelle cried. The plate missed the tray and landed in her lap. An uneaten slice of pizza slid onto her brand-new shorts. Facedown.

Michelle leaped up. Her shorts were spotted with pizza sauce and globs of sticky cheese.

"Ugh!" she cried. But Stephanie was long gone, strolling around the mess hall, chatting with Parker.

"Michelle, your shorts are ruined!" Mallory exclaimed.

"It was Stephanie's fault," Courtney said. "I saw the whole thing!"

Michelle fumed as she and her friends led the cleanup. They took the trays from every table and dumped the garbage in the appropriate bins. *Stephanie is completely out of con-*

trol, Michelle thought. *Someone should really teach her a lesson.*

When all the tables were cleared, Cal called for order.

"We need to vote on carnival booths now," he announced. "I'll read off a list of ideas that your counselors came up with. But feel free to come up with other ideas of your own."

Michelle barely paid attention. It was hard to think about fun and games and carnival events. All she could think about was how mean Stephanie was acting.

Stephanie scurried back to the table.

Michelle glared at her.

She acts like such a big boss, Michelle thought in disgust. *A big* mean *boss!*

"I really like the miniature golf idea," Stephanie was saying. "But maybe we should have a body-art booth. That's always fun. We could paint temporary tattoos, and spray kids' hair with glitter paint. I love to do that."

"Oh, I don't know," Mallory told her. "We've done that stuff at other fairs and carnivals."

"Yeah. Can't we come up with a different idea for this carnival?" Courtney added. "One *we* like?"

"I was just trying to give you a suggestion. I don't know why you're all being so—" Stephanie sighed. "Why don't you talk it over. I'll be back in a minute."

Michelle watched Stephanie hurry over to talk to her friend Tracy. "Well, you guys, which booth do you think we should have?" Michelle asked.

Mallory had a wild look in her eyes—and a big grin across her face.

"What is it?" Michelle asked her.

Mallory waved Michelle and the others closer. "I just had the most amazing idea," she said. "The perfect practical joke to pull on Stephanie!"

"Really?" Michelle said.

"Let's have a dunking tank," Mallory exclaimed. "Then we could trick Stephanie into being the one who gets dunked!"

Michelle imagined her sister plunging into a huge tank full of water. She imagined her dripping wet, wringing water out of her clothes and hair. She imagined her fuming with anger.

It was totally harmless, but embarrassing.

I like this idea, she thought.

"We could all take turns dunking her." Courtney giggled. "It's perfect!"

"Let's do it," Michelle declared.

"Wait a minute," Shari said. "Are you sure you want to, Michelle? I mean, Stephanie *is* your sister."

"Sister or not, someone's got to teach her a lesson," Michelle replied. She slapped a high-five with Mallory. "We'll show her she can't push us around."

"All right!" Mallory cheered.

Stephanie returned from Tracy's table. Michelle told her they had decided on which booth to have.

"A dunking booth?" Stephanie frowned. "Doesn't that seem a little mean-spirited?"

"The carnival is supposed to be fun for us, and this is what we want our booth to be," Mallory told her. "You don't want to fight with us, do you?"

Stephane hesitated. "No," she finally answered. "I really don't want to fight with any of you. A dunking booth will be fine."

Stephanie sighed. Michelle thought she looked tired—and maybe a little sad. For a split second she almost felt sorry for Stephanie. But then she remembered how mean Stephanie had been acting. No way. She wouldn't feel sorry for Stephanie at all.

"Anyway, I have an announcement to make," Stephanie continued. "Tonight's bonfire starts at seven-thirty. You have free time until then. But don't forget to go back to the bunk to get your sleeping bags. Bring them to the bonfire."

"Why? Are we sleeping outside?" Allison asked.

"No," Stephanie replied. "But you'll want to fold up the bags to sit on as cushions. And it can get pretty cool here at night. You might want to use them as blankets, too."

"Okay," Allison said.

Sleeping bags? Michelle thought. *Hmmmm.*

A nasty idea crossed Michelle's mind. One that would totally teach Stephanie that she couldn't be mean to her campers and expect to get away with it.

Plus, it was something Michelle's new friends would totally be into. Mallory would think she was so cool if she went through with it.

Yes! she decided. She'd do it!

"Oh, Stephanie," Michelle called. "If you want, I'll get your sleeping bag for you. Then you won't have to walk all the way back to the bunk."

"That would be great," Stephanie said. "Thanks, Michelle. I'll see you later."

Stephanie hurried to join her friend Tracy. Mallory poked Michelle.

"Why did you offer to do her a favor?" she asked. "I thought you were mad at her."

"I *am* mad," Michelle agreed. "And I definitely want to get Stephanie's sleeping bag for her."

A confused look crossed Mallory's face.

"You'll see why," Michelle told her. "And believe me, you're going to love it!"

STEPHANIE

Chapter
9

Stephanie stared into the wood shack in dismay.

Do they really need all this firewood for one bonfire? she wondered.

The small shed was stacked from floor to ceiling with logs of all sizes. She glanced at her watch and sighed. The bonfire was scheduled to start soon. And there was no sign of Cal. He had implied that the two of them were going to transport the wood together. Should she wait for him?

No, she decided. It would impress him if she was already hard at work when he got there.

She reached down and lifted up an armload of logs.

Ugh! The logs were heavier than they looked—and messy. Gooey strands of sap oozed out and stuck to her shirt and shorts. Bits of bark flaked off and tangled in her hair.

She dumped the wood into an empty wheelbarrow.

There was still so much left!

She glanced down the dirt road that led to the picnic grounds and the flagpole. No sign of Cal.

Maybe he had had an emergency or something, Stephanie thought. The bonfire was supposed to start soon. She hoped he was still going to come.

Another half hour went by and Stephanie's arms ached. She was getting too tired to move much more wood. The wheelbarrow was full and she'd begun piling up logs next to it.

Wasn't Cal ever going to show up? Stephanie caught something out of the corner of her eye.

What's that? she thought. She turned her

87

head sharply in the direction of the flagpole. Smoke. Definitely! Then she heard voices singing. She was missing the bonfire!

Parker had specified that Stephanie had to have the wood to the bonfire by the time it started! She had to move, she realized.

Stephanie grabbed the handles of the wheelbarrow. It was so heavy she couldn't move it!

Now what? she wondered.

She tried agian. Definitely too heavy. She sighed. And started unloading. Finally the wheelbarrow was light enough for her to push, and she headed toward the bonfire.

She felt awful. Her arms and legs were scratched by the firewood. Her back ached from the heavy work. And the night had turned cold. She shivered in her thin shirt and shorts.

Why had everything on this trip become so hard? Somehow, no matter what she did, Stephanie always found herself messing up!

Stephanie's arm muscles strained with the effort of pushing the cart. Tears of frustration sprang to her eyes as she trudged along the dusty dirt road.

Whether she was missing meetings, making her campers mad at her, or not getting her duties accomplished on time, one thing was sure: Everything Stephanie did showed Cal what a major loser she was.

All right, get a grip, she coached herself. *On top of everything else, you don't want anyone to think you're a crybaby.* She placed the wheelbarrow down for a second and took a deep breath.

Stephanie picked up the handles of the wheelbarrow and moved forward around a bend in the road. There was a clear view of the bonfire. The campers were sitting in a ring around the bonfire with their CITs.

Stephanie spotted Cal.

He sat cross-legged, leading a song and waving a toasted marshmallow in the air.

Parker sat next to him.

Stephanie couldn't believe her eyes. Had Cal been at the bonfire the whole time? Wasn't he supposed to help her? Even if he had forgotten about helping, shouldn't he wonder where she'd been?

Stephanie dropped the wheelbarrow and

stood staring. She shivered in the cool air. *This is unreal!* she thought angrily.

She stormed across the field and marched up to Cal and Parker. "Hey, what's going on?" she demanded.

Parker laughed. "Stephanie! You have dirt all over your face! What were you doing?"

Stephanie forced herself to remain calm. "I've been loading firewood for the past hour! Like you asked me to."

Cal looked at Parker. "I thought *you* were going to help with the firewood," he said.

Stephanie's mouth hung open. *Parker* was supposed to help her? Not Cal?

The whole time she was hauling those awful logs, getting filthy and practically breaking her back, *Parker* was supposed to be helping?

She clenched her fists. She'd never felt so angry in her whole life!

"You must have worked really hard," Cal added. "And as it turns out, we don't even need any extra wood."

"*You don't?*" Stephanie felt her voice rising. "I carted it all this way for *nothing?*" she shrieked.

"Oh, Stephanie, I'm so sorry," Parker said in an ultra-sweet voice. She turned to Cal, looking totally apologetic. "I was on my way to help her, but then I had a problem with a sick camper in bunk seven. I had to handle that situation first. So Stephanie stepped in and offered to take over. All by herself."

Cal grinned at Stephanie. "Wow. That was totally cool," he said.

Stephanie stared at Cal, then at Parker, then at Cal again. She didn't know what to say.

She was fuming mad. Parker had tricked her into doing all the work by herself. And now they didn't even need the firewood!

Parker was also giving Stephanie all the credit—and making her look good in front of Cal. Stephanie couldn't help but wonder, was Parker her friend—or not? If she wasn't a friend, why was she pretending to be one?

"Boy, Stephanie, you look beat." Cal broke the silence. "Why don't you get your sleeping bag and sit over here?" He patted the ground beside him. "The sing-along is winding down, but there are still some marshmallows left. I'll toast you a Cal Mason Special!"

Stephanie felt her anger melting away. Cal wanted her to sit with him? And he'd toast her a marshmallow? Maybe he didn't think she was a total loser after all.

It was the best news she'd had all day.

"Sure," she said. She hoped she didn't look as excited as she felt.

She nearly raced around the bonfire to where the Grape Jammers were sitting with the Bananna Boats.

"Stephanie, where were you?" Michelle asked.

"You don't want to know," Stephanie told her. "Did you bring my sleeping bag?"

"Right here!" Michelle lifted the dark green bag. Stephanie grabbed it. Then she noticed the strange look on Michelle's face— and Mallory's, too. It was as if they were trying not to laugh.

What's their problem? Stephanie wondered. Then she thought, *Who cares? Cal's waiting for me. I don't have time for this right now.*

She hurried away. Thankfully, Cal was still saving a spot for her.

"Here I am," she told him. She unzipped the sleeping bag halfway and slid her legs inside. It felt so cozy. The heat from the campfire warmed the rest of her. She stopped shivering and began to enjoy herself.

Cal lifted a long stick out of the fire. He put together a sandwhich of toasted marshmallows with small bits of chocolate between two graham crackers. "Here you go!" he said, handing the treat to Stephanie. "Hope you like s'mores."

"Mmmmm! Delicious," Stephanie said. The marshmallows were crisp on the outside and gooey on the inside—just the way she liked them. The chocolate melted and oozed between them.

Stephanie reached down with one hand and scratched her leg inside her sleeping bag. *Hmm,* she thought. *Must be a mosquito bite.*

Then her other leg began to itch, too. She popped the rest of the s'more into her mouth and dug the fingernails of both hands into her skin.

She scratched and scratched. But for some reason, the itching got worse. It itched so much, it burned.

"What's wrong with you?" Parker asked, staring at her.

Stephanie leaned forward and scratched even harder. "I . . . don't know," she gasped. "I guess I got bit at the wood shack."

The itching and burning were so bad she couldn't stand it. She unzipped the sleeping bag and kicked it away from her legs.

"Are you okay?" Cal asked. He stared at her, too.

"I'm just . . . all bit up," she managed to say. She stood up and started hopping from leg to leg, scratching furiously.

She knew she looked ridiculous, but she couldn't help it. All she wanted was for the itch to go away.

Parker giggled. "What is that? Some kind of Native American s'mores dance?"

"No!" Stephanie exclaimed. "This is . . . it's . . ." All she could concentrate on was the itch. She had to make it stop!

She glanced down at the unzipped sleeping bag. Dusty white powder was smeared all over the lining.

Itching powder, she thought. Tears welled

in her eyes. Who would do that to her? Who would put itching powder . . .

She heard a noise from the other end of the bonfire—a giggle. Her eyes followed it to the Grape Jammers. Michelle and the others were staring at her and laughing.

"Would you excuse me, please?" she muttered to Cal and Parker.

She raced around the bonfire and stopped in front of the Grape Jammers. "You did this to me!" she declared, scratching her legs.

"Did what?" Michelle asked.

Mallory laughed out loud. Shari, Courtney, Jeannie, and Allison all giggled.

Stephanie felt a tear slide down her cheek. She wiped it away with the back of her hand before anyone could see it.

She felt dumbfounded. Michelle had just ruined the best moment she'd had since she got to camp! She felt her face get hot.

"You are all in big, *huge* trouble!" she said.

"Oh, come on, Stephanie." Michelle grinned. "It was just a little practical joke."

"It wasn't funny!" Stephanie snapped. "Not at all!"

"Well, you deserved it," Michelle shot

back. "You're the meanest counselor in the world."

Stephanie's breath caught in her throat. How could Michelle say that? Especially when all she'd been trying to do was follow the rules and make everybody happy.

Stephanie ripped her sneaker off and scratched the bottom of her foot.

Well, now I don't care if they do think I'm the meanest counselor in the world. I'm through making everybody happy. I'm through being nice! Completely and totally through!

MICHELLE

Chapter
10

Michelle yawned. "I don't feel like playing volleyball," she complained. "I feel like taking a nap." She collapsed onto a bleacher seat next to Mallory.

"I'm tired, too," Mallory added. "And it's all Stephanie's fault."

"You're right," Jeannie agreed. "I still can't believe she made us wash her sleeping bag, her sheets, and all her clothes last night. *Before* she'd let us go to bed."

"Yeah, I mean, we told her we didn't put itching powder in anything but the sleeping bag," Shari commented.

Michelle and her friends stared across the

sports field. It was crowded that morning. The counselors had set up six volleyball nets for a campwide tournament. The Grape Jammers were supposed to play the Apple Dumplings.

"I'm so tired, I can't even *lift* a volleyball," Courtney wailed.

"Your sister is too mean, Michelle," Shari said. "How are we going to make it through the rest of the week with her as our CIT?"

Everyone looked at Michelle. "Hey, it's not my fault she turned into Stephanie the Witch," she said.

"You mean Stephanie the *Itch*," Mallory joked.

Michelle burst out laughing. Shari, Jeannie, Courtney, and Mallory joined in.

"This is only the beginning of our revenge," Mallory decided. "We're going to have to play more jokes."

"Like last night's," Jeannie chimed in. "Watching Stephanie hop up and down was worth having to wash all her clothes."

"Definitely!" Courtney agreed.

"Uh . . ." Michelle started to protest.

Michelle wasn't so sure she liked playing

practical jokes. Even if the person deserved them. They just seemed too—cruel.

"Don't look now," Shari whispered. "But Stephanie is flying by on her broomstick!"

Michelle glanced up. Stephanie and her friend Tracy were heading toward them, the Apple Dumplings trailing behind.

"Let's go, you guys!" Stephanie called out. "It's time for your first match."

Michelle groaned as she stood up.

The Apple Dumplings took their positions on the grass court. The Grape Jammers took their places across the net. Michelle was first to serve the ball.

Tweeeet!

Stephanie blew her whistle to start the game. Michelle swung her right arm to serve the ball.

"Yeoouch!" She let out a yell.

Stephanie ran to her. "Michelle, are you okay?" she asked.

Michelle winced. "I think I hurt my shoulder."

"Maybe you should go see the nurse," Stephanie suggested.

"It doesn't hurt that much," Michelle told her.

"Well, I have an ice pack," Stephanie said. "Why don't you sit out this game and put some ice on your shoulder."

"Okay. Sure." Michelle shrugged and walked off the field. Her shoulder really didn't hurt too badly. The ice would probably take care of it.

She took a seat in the bleachers and held the ice pack to her shoulder. She watched Stephanie running back and forth, coaching the game.

Boy, she's really into this stuff, Michelle thought. *Stephanie really could make a decent counselor. Especially if she concentrated on her campers instead of on impressing Parker and Cal.*

"Excuse me!"

Michelle turned and spotted Parker crossing the field, heading toward her. Parker smiled a sickly sweet smile at Michelle.

"Do me a favor, okay?" Parker asked.

"What is it?" Michelle wanted to know.

"Nothing major," Parker continued in her fake-sweet tone. She held out a stack of papers and peeled one off the top. She handed it to Michelle.

"It's a map of campsites, for the camp out tonight," Parker explained. "It shows where each of the bunks will be." She pointed out the girls section and the boys section.

"Just give this map to Stephanie. Okay?" Parker marched off before Michelle had a chance to say a word.

What a phoney-baloney, Michelle thought. *I can't believe Stephanie hasn't caught on to her by now.*

Michelle glanced at the map. The different campsites were clearly marked. She found the Grape Jammers' site in the girls section.

The boys section was a short distance away. That's where she spotted Cal's name.

I bet Stephanie would do anything to camp right next to Cal, she thought with a giggle. *That is, if Parker let Stephanie anywhere near Cal.*

Mallory jogged off the field.

"Aren't you supposed to be playing volleyball?" Michelle asked.

"Don't worry," Mallory joked. "Our team is much better off without me. I stink at volleyball." She glanced at the piece of paper in Michelle's hand. "Hey! What's that?"

"It's the map we're supposed to use to find our campsite tonight. Parker just gave it to me," Michelle explained.

"I saw you giggling. What's so funny?" Mallory asked.

"I was just thinking about how Stephanie would give anything to have our campsite right next to Cal's," she answered.

"Oh, wow!" Mallory exclaimed. "Michelle, you're a genius!"

Michelle sat up straight in her seat. "Huh? What are you talking about?"

Michelle could hear Stephanie coaching the Grape Jammers. "That's it, Shari," she called out. "Spike it!"

Mallory waited till Stephanie was on the other side of the field. "I have just come up with the most awesome practical joke idea *ever!*" she continued.

"What is it?" Michelle whispered.

"Let's tell Stephanie that Cal wants to meet her tonight at his campsite," Mallory said.

"Why would we do that?" Michelle demanded.

"Because Stephanie will need to use this map to get from our campsite to Cal's," Mallory explained. "But you and I will change the map! Stephanie will get totally lost."

Michelle frowned. "Wait a minute. I don't want her to go anywhere dangerous. . . ."

"She won't," Mallory assured her. "I know these woods better than anybody at camp." She glanced down at the map and grabbed Michelle's pencil.

She quickly scribbled a few lines on the map. "This will definitely have her going in circles for a while. She'll be totally safe, but also totally confused."

That's not so bad, Michelle reasoned. *Stephanie can't get into too much trouble going in circles.*

Mallory grinned. She slapped Michelle on the back. "You are a genius! After tonight the two of us will go down in practical-joke history!"

Tweet!

Stephanie's annoying whistle pierced Michelle's eardrums. "Okay, Grape Jammers!" she called. "Good job! Hang out on the sidelines until your next game."

Mallory finished changing the map, and Michelle slipped it into her pocket. "Go to it, Michelle!" Mallory cheered. She headed over to the sidelines, leaving Michelle on the bleachers.

Stephanie jogged over to where Michelle was sitting. "How's the shoulder?" she asked.

"It feels better," Michelle reported. She fished the map out of her pocket.

"What's that?" Stephanie wanted to know.

"It's a map for the camp out tonight," Michelle told her. "It shows where all the campsites are. Parker gave it to me to give to you."

"Oh, okay. Thanks." Stephanie shoved the map in her pocket and turned to go back to the game.

Michelle hesitated. No, she realized. She had to do it. She had to go through with the joke.

"Wait!" Michelle told her. "Parker gave me a message, too. She said it was really important."

"Okay, tell me," Stephanie snapped. "But make it fast."

She took a deep breath. "Cal really likes you!" Michelle blurted out. "Parker said that he's dying to spend time alone with you."

Stephanie gasped. "No way!"

"Way," Michelle replied. "He wants you

to meet him at his campsite tonight. After we all go to sleep."

"But I can't!" Stephanie wailed. "I have to stay with you guys." She looked totally upset. "Plus, I don't know my way around the campsites. Especially in the dark."

"Oh, brother," Michelle muttered. "I guess you don't care about Cal the way he cares about you."

"I *do* care," Stephanie insisted. "But how can I meet him?"

Michelle rolled her eyes. "Simple. You ask Tracy to watch us. You use your map to find Cal's campsite. And you take a flashlight to see in the dark."

Stephanie's eyes began to sparkle. "Michelle, you're a genius! I'll do it!" She threw the volleyball back to the Grape Jammers and raced off to talk to Tracy.

From the other end of the field, Mallory gave Michelle a thumbs-up. Michelle returned it. She wanted to smile, but for some reason, she couldn't.

If this is the greatest practical joke in history, Michelle wondered, *how come I'm not laughing?*

STEPHANIE

Chapter 11

Stephanie couldn't stop thinking about Cal. She thought about him all during the volley-ball matches that day.

She thought about him as she and the other CITs helped pack cookout bags in the kitchen late that afternoon.

She thought about him as the Grape Jammers got ready for the big overnight in the woods.

All she could think about was Cal. He was so adorable and friendly and nice. And he liked her!

If one thing in this whole crummy camp turned out for the best, Stephanie was glad it might be her and Cal getting together!

One Boss Too Many

Just as she was gathering the Grape Jammers together to start on their hike, Cal came striding past.

"Hey, Stephanie!" he called. "I was hoping we could spend some time together and talk."

"Really? Sure! I mean, I know," she corrected herself. *Why did I say that?* she wondered. *I sound like an idiot!*

Cal grinned at her and waved. She watched him walk away. He was so cool. She was so lucky he liked her!

"Hey, you're daydreaming again," a voice called out.

"Huh?" Stephanie blinked.

Tracy hurried up to her, grinning. The Apple Dumplings were lined up behind her, getting ready to hike the trail that led through the woods.

"You're smiling like crazy. Are you still thinking about tonight?" Tracy asked.

"I can't help it," Stephanie told her. "But I have to admit, I feel bad leaving my campers. Are you sure you can check on them tonight?"

"No problem," Tracy assured her. "The

CITs will all get together after the kids are asleep, anyway. We can all take turns checking on your group."

"Great," Stephanie said. "But do me a favor? Could *you* check my group. I don't want the other CITs to know. After all, I really shouldn't be doing this."

"No, you've *got* to do this," Tracy told her. "Meeting Cal—that is *so* cool!"

"I know," Stephanie said. She couldn't stop a smile from spreading across her face.

Stephanie and Tracy split up to lead their groups along the trail. Parker and the other counselors led the other groups. It was a short hike, and pretty easy. Finally they reached a big clearing in the middle of the woods.

"This is the girls campsite," Parker announced. "We'll build our main campfire here. And we'll have our cookout together. Later, we'll split up into bunks."

Everyone unloaded supplies for the cookout. It was fun to cook over an open fire, but Stephanie could barely pay attention. Her food might as well have been sawdust, because she wasn't tasting it.

One Boss Too Many

She couldn't wait for night to come so she could meet Cal.

Finally the cookout was over. After cleaning up, each group hiked a little farther into the woods to find a cozy clearing to pitch camp in.

First they built a campfire—smaller than the one for the cookout. Then the Grape Jammers shook out their sleeping bags and arranged them in a circle around the campfire.

They all sang songs for a while. Then Stephanie told them it was time to turn in. She waited while they talked quietly.

They are really acting like angels tonight, Stephanie thought in surprise. *Maybe they're finally seeing how hard I'm working—and they're giving me a break. Or maybe they just decided to stop complaining and have a good time.*

She sat on her own sleeping bag and gazed up at the stars. It was a great night for a camp out. Clear and warm.

It was a perfect night to meet Cal.

Finally everything was quiet. All the girls had gone to sleep. Stephanie piled more firewood on the fire. Then she fished her hairbrush from her backpack. She wished she had thought to bring a mirror.

She fixed her hair as best she could. Then she pulled on her warm-up jacket and grabbed the map.

"Hey, how's it going?"

Stephanie glanced behind her. Tracy appeared. Right on time.

"All set," Stephanie whispered back.

"Okay. See you later," Tracy told her. "Have fun!"

"I'll be back really soon," Stephanie replied. "I promise."

Excitedly, she headed for Cal's campsite. According to the map, it was very close by.

She easily found the path. It began by a tree marked with a red metal triangle that glowed in the dark. She took out her flashlight and aimed it at the ground. She followed the path steadily for a few minutes. Then the path forked in two directions.

She paused to study the map. She needed to find a second tree with another red marker and turn left.

She found the tree, turned, and followed

the path. A few yards away the path suddenly ended.

"That's strange," Stephanie muttered. She aimed her flashlight through the trees. There wasn't any clearing ahead.

She shined her flashlight around the woods. In the distance, she could see a few campfires going. There were definitely other campers out there, but which campsite was Cal's?

She checked the map again. It led her away from the path and through the trees and bushes.

She sighed. She would just have to make her own path.

Twigs snapped under her sneakers. Branches poked her in the ribs and scratched her skin. Still, she kept on trudging through the woods.

This really hurts! she thought. *But when I find Cal—it will be worth a little discomfort!*

Something reached out and grabbed her.

She gasped and spun around.

Oh! She let out a breath. *It's just some ivy, caught on my jacket!*

She let out a nervous laugh and pushed on. Why couldn't she see any campfires?

She shined the flashlight down at her watch. Yikes! It was getting late. She'd been walking for almost a half hour.

I wasn't supposed to leave my campers alone this long, she worried. *I hope Tracy doesn't mind! I hope Parker doesn't check our campsite and find me gone.*

Her pulse started pounding. She hadn't realized so many things could go wrong. What if Cal didn't wait for her? What if he was mad because she couldn't find him?

She paused to catch her breath. She shined her flashlight through the woods. Nothing. No sign of a campfire. No sounds at all.

Worrying about Tracy or Cal wasn't her worst problem, she suddenly realized.

My worst problem is—I'm completely lost!

MICHELLE

Chapter
12

"She's gone," Michelle announced. She watched Tracy leave the Grape Jammers' campsite to check in on her own campers.

One by one, her friends sat up.

"This is going to be so good!" Mallory exclaimed. She rubbed her hands together.

"Mallory, this *is* a truly excellent plan," Courtney added.

"I wish I could see Stephanie's face when she realizes she's lost," Shari said. She and Allison and Jeannie burst out laughing.

"It's too bad we can't follow her," Mallory said. "Then we *could* see her face."

"But then our campsite would be empty," Courtney said.

"Yeah, and that would be even funnier," Michelle added. "Stephanie would realize she's lost, come back here, and find us gone! She'd flip out." She chuckled.

Mallory stared at Michelle. "Once again, that is a totally brilliant idea, Michelle!" she exclaimed. "You're getting to be a better practical joker than me."

"What are you talking about?" Michelle asked.

"We *should* disappear," Mallory said. "We should move to another campsite. Imagine how confused Stephanie would be then!"

"Wow," Courtney said. "She would go completely crazy."

"We could pack up really fast," Mallory said. "We only have our sleeping bags and backpacks."

"Michelle, I don't know how you come up with these amazing ideas!" Shari gushed.

Everyone praised Michelle, slapping her high-fives.

I worked really hard to make these friends, Michelle thought. *And now they think I'm totally cool for coming up with this stuff. If I tell them I don't want to do it, they'll think I'm a nerd.*

And maybe they won't want to be friends with me anymore.

"All right, let's do it!" Michelle exclaimed.

The Grape Jammers rolled up their sleeping bags and packed their backpacks.

"Where should we move to?" Shari asked.

"Just to the next campsite over," Mallory replied. "It's empty."

"Do you think we'll get in trouble?" Courtney asked. She and Allison exchanged a worried look.

"How?" Mallory asked. "Everyone's sleeping. Nobody will know we're gone except Stephanie. And she can't tell—or she'll get herself into trouble for leaving us alone!"

"Mallory, you are still the queen of the practical jokers," Michelle told her.

Michelle led the way out of the campsite. Once on the path, Mallory took over. They followed her through the woods, aiming their flashlights at the ground.

Soon their path narrowed. Tree branches snapped against Michelle's arms and legs. She bent her head to look at the sky. The trees were so thick, they blocked the light from the moon. She couldn't even see any stars.

Michelle imagined Stephanie's face when she found the empty campsite. It *was* pretty funny.

They walked for several more minutes.

"Aren't we there yet?" Courtney asked.

"Yeah. I'm tired. I want to get some sleep," Shari complained.

"I thought you said the empty campsite was nearby," Jeannie pointed out. "We should be there by now."

Mallory didn't answer.

"Uh—Mallory?" Michelle asked.

Mallory stopped walking. She turned around.

Even in the dim light, Michelle noticed a strange expression on her friend's face. "Uh, I'm a little confused," she admitted. "I wish Stephanie didn't have the map."

"Why? I thought you said you knew these woods better than anyone!" Michelle felt a stab of alarm.

"Uh—I thought I did," Mallory said.

Michelle didn't like the tone of Mallory's voice. She sounded nervous.

"Don't worry, guys," Mallory assured them. "The campsites are all really close together. We'll find one of them, and then I'll know exactly where we are."

"How will we find a campsite? I can't even see another campfire," Michelle said. She peered into the dark woods. The trees seemed a bit taller than before. The sky seemed darker.

She shivered.

"What if all the campfires went out?" Courtney asked. "It's late. It's not like anyone would be tending them." She moved closer to Michelle.

"Maybe we should yell for help," Shari added.

"No!" Mallory said. "Don't yell. What if a counselor hears us? Then we'll definitely get into trouble. You know we're not supposed to leave our campsite."

"Okay, everybody, stop worrying," Michelle said. "Mallory knows where we are. She just needs to find something familiar."

"How is she going to find anything familiar when it's so dark out?" Courtney asked.

There was an uncomfortable silence.

"I think we should go back to our campsite," Michelle blurted out.

"Me, too," Courtney agreed.

"No way! If we go back, we won't trick Stephanie," Mallory insisted.

That's it, Michelle realized. *This has gone far enough. Now somebody has to put a stop to this.*

"We already tricked her by changing the map." Michelle spoke up. "I think that's enough."

"Michelle!" Mallory looked upset. "We all agreed to switch campsites."

"Yeah, but now we know it was a bad idea," Michelle said.

"Are you wimping out on us?" Mallory asked. "What's the deal, Michelle? Do you turn into a nerd at the stroke of midnight?"

"Hey, it sounded like a good idea," Michelle defended herself. "But I think we've gone too far. Now we'd better head back."

"All right," Mallory challenged. "Let's vote on it. Everyone who's with me, raise your hands."

Mallory raised her hand. She glanced around at the rest of the group. Nobody budged.

Michelle broke the silence. "Everyone who wants to go back?"

All the Grape Jammers except Mallory raised their hands.

Mallory bowed her head. The girls turned and started walking in the direction they had come from. Michelle threw an arm around Mallory's shoulders. "Listen, Mallory. Sometimes practical jokes can go too far. Especially when they'll hurt the people you're playing them on."

"Yeah. I guess," Mallory said slowly.

Michelle knew Mallory wanted everyone to believe she was upset. But she had a funny feeling that Mallory was actually relieved to be going back to camp, too. Only she didn't know how to admit it.

Michelle shined her flashlight at a blue trail marker. "Wait a minute. I'm confused. Did we pass a blue marker on the way over here?"

Mallory took a long look at the marker. "I don't think so. I didn't see it before," she finally said.

"So what does that mean?" Michelle asked.

Mallory took a deep breath. "Uh, I think

it means we may have walked a tiny bit in the wrong direction."

"How tiny a bit?" Courtney demanded.

"Actually—a lot." Mallory swallowed hard.

Michelle stared at her. "You know, Mallory, I'm beginning to think we just played the most awful practical joke—on ourselves!"

Chapter
13

This *can't* be the right way!" Stephanie muttered. She held up the map and shined her flashlight on it.

"This is useless," she said, her voice cracking slightly.

It was too dark to see any of the landmarks on the map. Like the giant boulder that was supposed to be off to her right. Or the marshy pond that should have been on her left.

All she could see was the ground directly in front of her if she aimed her flashlight directly down. When she did *that*, though, the rest of the woods were plunged into total, complete darkness.

I never knew it could be so, so spooky at night, she thought.

Something rustled in the bushes to her right. She let out a little squeal and jumped back. Stumbling over a twisted root, she nearly fell. She reached out to grab something to hold on to. Thorny branches scratched her hand.

"Oww!" she exclaimed.

Where is Cal's campsite? she wondered. *And why did I ever believe this stupid map? Why would a reliable map tell you to leave a trail, anyway? Now I couldn't find my way back to the path for all the money in the world.*

Her heart felt heavy. *I'll never find Cal now. And it's late, and Tracy will be frantic. I'll get in big trouble for nothing. And Cal will think I don't like him, and . . .*

A knot formed in her throat.

Okay, okay, calm down, she told herself. *It won't do any good to get all upset.*

She took a deep breath and reached up to tuck her long hair back behind her ears.

Ugh! There were damp leaves tangled in her hair. And something gooey. Tree sap. Eeew!

It took a couple of minutes to free her hair from the sticky sap. Then she aimed the flashlight down on her clothes.

Her jacket and jeans were smeared with drying sap and dirt. Her best sneakers were filthy.

Oh, who cares? she thought. *I'm cold and dirty . . . I just want to find a campfire—any campfire!*

Suddenly she smelled smoke.

And where there's smoke, there's a campfire! she thought.

She peered through the trees. Yes!

About a hundred yards ahead, she could spot the flickering light of someone's campfire. She felt her heart leap in excitement.

"Thank goodness!" she exclaimed.

She pushed her way through the underbrush again. The closer she drew to the light, the thicker the branches around her seemed to grow. Each step was more difficult than the one before.

Finally she stumbled into a clearing. "Hello? Anyone here?" she called. She hurried toward the campfire.

Somebody was just about to eat. Hamburger and hot dog buns sat neatly on a cooler nearby. Several bottles of cola sat waiting on a blanket by the fire.

She sniffed the air. It smelled like apples and cinnamon. Whoever made the fire must have thrown in some incense, too.

"Hello?" she called again. "I got separated from my group and—"

The cuff of her jeans snagged on a spikey tree stump. She groaned in frustration and yanked her leg free.

Riiiiip!

A giant hole appeared in her jeans. She lost her balance and flew forward, her arms whirling like propellers as she tried to catch her balance.

"Stephanie?" a voice asked in surprise.

"Cal?"

Her jaw fell open. This was *Cal's* campsite? She actually *found* it?

Then it hit her—if this was Cal's campsite, then this romantic cookout must be for *her!*

And I look a total mess! She reached up to smooth her hair, but it was no use. She was not a pretty sight.

"Wow, Cal!" she said. "This looks amazing! I didn't expect you to go to all this trouble just for me." She gestured at the food and sodas. "And I love that incense," she added.

Cal scrunched up his nose. "Incense? It's bug repellent."

"Oh. Well, it's nice anyway," Stephanie said.

"Stephanie, what are you doing here?" Cal asked. "And what happened to you?"

Stephanie stared at him. "You *asked* me to come," she replied. "Once the kids were asleep."

Cal's eyes widened. "You left your campers asleep—alone—at your campsite?"

Stephanie gulped. "Um, no, not at all! Tracy is watching them for me. Because you said you wanted to see me tonight."

"I don't remember saying that," Cal said. "I said I wanted to talk to you later. But not later *tonight*." Cal acted uncomfortable.

Stephanie got a weird feeling in the pit of her stomach. "You didn't tell Parker that you wanted me to meet you? Alone?" She stopped. She decided to leave out the part where Parker said Cal liked her.

"B-but, what about the hot dogs and the sodas?" she asked instead.

"The senior staff is getting together," Cal replied. "Because the junior staff is supposed to be with the campers." He frowned in disapproval.

"Oh." Stephanie dropped her eyes to the ground. "I guess . . . I didn't realize how late it was . . . and, I, uh—"

Cal cleared his throat. "Stephanie," he began slowly, "I'm sorry if you thought that I was asking for a date or something."

There was a sudden rustling in the woods. Parker and three other senior counselors stepped into the campsite.

Parker blinked at Stephanie. And burst into laughter. "Oh, wow!" she cried. "Is that the new 'great outdoors' look?"

The other counselors laughed, too.

Stephanie felt her cheeks flush in embarrassment. For a friend, Parker was sure having a good laugh at her expense.

"Stephanie was helping me collect twigs and branches for our cookout," Cal quickly told the others.

"At midnight?" Parker didn't look convinced. "Why is she here so late, anyway?"

She paused. "Stephanie, you didn't leave your campers *alone*, did you?" Parker's voice rose. "Cal, I'm shocked! I certainly thought Stephanie would know better! She—"

"Calm down, Parker," Cal said. "Stephanie had Tracy take care of her group. And she's on her way back now."

Stephanie flashed him a grateful smile. "Sorry about the mix-up," she said. "I'll see you tomorrow."

She turned to flee, but realized she had no idea how to get back to her campsite.

"Uh, Cal, could you . . ."

"No problem," Cal said. He showed her where the path was. "Follow the trail. At the second red marker, turn right and your campsite is just ahead."

Stephanie plunged into the woods. She practically ran down the path.

What a horrible night! She cringed as she remembered the look of surprise on Cal's face. And how Parker and the others laughed at her.

I've never been so humiliated in my life! she

thought. *Cal probably thinks I'm a total jerk. And Parker—she's not my friend at all. She told Michelle that Cal liked me, when he really didn't.*

If only she hadn't listened to Michelle. If only—

Michelle!

She stopped dead in her tracks. Michelle was the one who told her to meet Cal. Michelle was the one who said that Parker said that Cal said . . .

She tricked me! Stephanie's mouth dropped open in surprise. Another practical joke!

She clamped her mouth shut and marched grimly toward the Grape Jammers' campsite. She wasn't far away now.

I will get her for this! Stephanie vowed.

She stepped into the campsite. The first thing she saw was her sleeping bag on the ground.

And a lot of empty space.

There were no other sleeping bags.

And no campers.

Chapter 14

Michelle stared into the dark woods surrounding them. She whirled around, then stared at Mallory. "We're lost!" she said. "Totally, completely lost!"

"Yes, we are!" Mallory exploded. "And it's not all my fault! We all wanted to move our campsite, not just me."

"I can't believe this!" Michelle exclaimed. The others gathered around her in alarm.

"What are we gong to do?" Courtney whined.

"I'm scared!" Allison added.

Michelle sighed. "Okay, everybody, calm down. Mallory is right, you know."

"I am?" Mallory seemed surprised.

"Sure," Michelle told her. "We did all agree to move our campsite." She shivered. It was cold out. And being lost in the woods was scarier than she wanted to admit.

But I can't let the others know I'm scared, she thought.

Michelle straightened her shoulders. "Listen, there's really nothing to be frightened of," she told Courtney. "We're together, aren't we?"

"Yeah," Shari said. "But we can't find our way back to camp."

"But we know we're not far away," Michelle pointed out. "I have a great idea! Let's set up a campsite right here."

"Here?" Shari exchanged a doubtful look with Courtney, Allison, and Jeannie.

"Sure. Why not?" Michelle replied. "We don't want to walk around in the woods all night. We'll camp here. What's the difference? We'll wake up early tomorrow. We could even find our way back to our old campsite before anyone knows we're missing."

They got themselves organized. They took their flashlights from their packs and

switched them on. With all of them carrying
the lights, it didn't seem very dark anymore.
Everyone spread their sleeping bags in a circle and shined their lights on each other.

"I don't think I can fall asleep," Courtney said.

"Me either," Allison admitted.

"Let's tell stories," Jeannie suggested.

"Great idea!" Mallory said. "Michelle, you
know the best stories. You go first!"

"Okay," Michelle said. She held the flashlight under her chin and shined the light on
her face. She spoke in a low, spooky voice.

"Once upon a time, there was a swamp
behind a school yard. All the kids knew
about it, but nobody had ever seen it. It was
forbidden."

"This is scary," Shari whispered excitedly.

"I love scary stories." Jeannie giggled.

Michelle continued. "One night, after a big
school dance, a few kids dared one another
to go and see the swamp. They left the school
yard and tiptoed through the dark, dark
woods. The swamp was in the middle of
the woods.

"Nobody wanted to go first," Michelle

went on. "Then one girl said she would go first. She pushed through the trees and the other kids followed her. The woods were dark and quiet."

"Like these woods!" Mallory whispered.

"They couldn't see anything. Then suddenly, they heard a scream!"

There was a rustling noise in the woods. The bushes parted and a large, dark form stepped into the campsite.

"The swamp creature!" Courtney yelled.

"Aaaahhhh!" Allison screamed.

Michelle's heart pounded. She spun around and shined her flashlight on the creature.

Stephanie!

"W-we thought you were the swamp creature!" Michelle let out a nervous giggle.

"Well, I'm not." Stephanie scowled at them. "But in a minute you're going to wish I were." She sat down in the circle of campers.

"Michelle, get that flashlight out of my face! Now tell me—what are you doing over here? Why did you move your campsite?"

Michelle and her friends exchanged guilty looks. Nobody said anything.

"I have just had the worst night of my entire life," Stephanie declared. "Thanks to you and your crummy practical jokes." She reached up to pull dry leaves and twigs out of her hair. "Plus, I was really worried when I couldn't find you at the campsite," she added. "And scared. I was terrified that something awful had happened to you!"

"Really?" Michelle frowned. It never occurred to her that Stephanie would get scared.

"We changed campsites to confuse you," Mallory admitted.

"But we ended up getting lost," Courtney added.

"I can't believe you would do such a dumb thing," Stephanie said. "I forgave you for the prank with the itching powder. But I don't think I can ever forgive you for this!"

"Well, you deserved it, you know!" Michelle blurted out. "You're so mean. You're like, the worst counselor ever!"

The others nodded in agreement.

"Yeah. You probably didn't really care that

we were missing," Courtney said. "You care about us only when there's work to do."

"Or when you want to impress Cal," Mallory put in.

"That's not true," Stephanie protested.

"Right. I'll bet she was worried," Michelle began.

Stephanie shot her a grateful look.

"Worried that all the chores wouldn't get done!" Michelle finished. She crossed her arms and glared at Stephanie.

The other girls laughed.

Stephanie looked stung. "I'm not that bad."

"Yes, you are," Michelle insisted. "You don't care how we feel. You care only about Cal. And Parker. And everyone knows what a snake in the grass Parker is."

"What? What do you mean, everyone knows?" Stephanie sank down on to a sleeping bag.

"It's true," Mallory added. "Everyone knows Parker is a total phony."

"My sister was in Parker's bunk last year," Courtney added. "Parker was the same way then. She made everyone else do all the work for her."

"Yeah," Mallory said. "Then, two years ago, there was this counselor who liked Cal. Parker made her do all sorts of stuff that would look like she messed up her duties. Parker did such a good job of making it look like the counselor messed up that Cal had to fire the counselor."

"But why would Parker want the counselor to be fired?" Stephanie asked.

"Duh," Michelle answered. "Because Parker likes Cal. She wants him all to herself."

A stunned look crossed Stephanie's face. "That's why," she mumbled to herself. "That's why she acts so friendly toward me one minute and so strange the next! Parker knows I like Cal, so she wants to get me fired!"

"Yeah. But even if that's the case, you could have been nice to us," Mallory added, glaring at Stephanie. "Instead of mean!"

Stephanie looked more upset than ever. "Wait. You guys knew about Parker all along and you never told me?" She stared at them in disbelief.

"I wanted to tell you, at first," Michelle admitted. "But then you were totally mean to me, Stephanie. You put me in charge, and that made me feel terrible. All you cared about was impressing Parker and Cal."

Michelle waited for Stephanie to start yelling and screaming.

To her surprise, Stephanie didn't yell or scream. "Wow. You all must really hate me," she said.

Michelle felt awful. "I don't hate you," she said. "You're still my sister."

"I was just trying to be a good counselor," Stephanie told the group.

"But good counselors can be nice," Michelle pointed out. "Everyone doesn't have to be like Parker."

Stephanie was silent. "You're right, Michelle," she said suddenly. "I let Parker push me around. I believed everything she told me. When she put me in a tough spot and gave me extra work, or when things went wrong, I took it out on you guys."

Michelle and the others exchanged surprised glances.

"I've been pretty mean to you guys,"

Stephanie said. "Parker set me up, and I fell for it. I'm really, really sorry."

Michelle's eyes widened. Stephanie was apologizing!

Yes! The old Stephanie was back! *This* was the sister Michelle knew and loved!

"Anyway, I promise to be the best counselor in the world from now on," Stephanie added.

"And, uh—we're sorry for pulling all those dumb pranks on you," Mallory offered.

"You are?" Stephanie asked.

"Well, Michelle did tell us how great you were," Mallory said. "We just didn't believe her."

Stephanie smiled at Michelle. "You did? You told everyone I was great?"

"Well, not the *whole* time," Michelle admitted. "I was pretty mad at you for a while."

Stephanie laughed. "I would have been mad at me, too!" she joked.

"Hey, I have an idea," Michelle said. "What if we forgive you for being a lousy counselor, and you forgive us for pulling our dumb pranks? We'll just start all over again!''

The girls stared at Stephanie, waiting for her answer.

Stephanie grinned. "Great idea, Michelle," she said. "But let's agree on one more thing. Something really important."

"What is it?" Michelle asked.

"Let's all agree to get Parker!"

Michelle looked at her friends. They nodded back to her.

"It's a deal," Michelle said. She glanced at Mallory. "And we know just how to do it."

STEPHANIE

Chapter
15

Okay, let's hear your idea!" Stephanie said.

She sat at the Grape Jammers' table in the mess hall the next morning. Parker wasn't anywhere nearby.

"Mallory has great ideas for practical jokes," Michelle added. "And this is her best yet. It's something we were planning to do to *you*, Stephanie."

Stephanie's eyes widened. "Really? Okay—spill!"

"Okay," Michelle replied. "We want to trick Parker into being the main attraction at the dunk tank at the carnival. Then we all get to take turns dunking her!"

"That's a great idea!"

Stephanie pictured Parker standing on the small piece of wood suspended above the large tank of water. Then she imagined herself grabbing a baseball and throwing it at the target next to the tank.

Yes! A direct hit, which will make Parker fall into the chilly water beneath her. When she surfaces, Parker's perfect hair will be matted to her perfect face! And she'll look like a drowned rat. Stephanie chuckled at the fantasy. It would be absolutely perfect.

"Uh-oh. Wait a minute," Stephanie said. "How do we get her into the tank?"

"She'd go if Cal asked her to do it," Mallory pointed out.

Stephanie grinned. *What an awesome idea! These girls are crafty! I'm sure glad they're on my side now!*

"Hey, that's a good idea," Courtney said. "What if we told Parker that Cal wants to see her, and trick her into the booth that way?"

"We'd need a better story than that," Mallory said.

"Yeah!" Michelle exclaimed. "Like, we'd have to tell her that Cal realized how much he likes her or something, and that he wants to see her so he can give her a big smooch."

Stephanie laughed. "Maybe that's a little too much. Cal's been ignoring Parker for so long, she might not believe us if we tell her that."

She thought for a moment. "Hey, I've got it!" she said. "How's this? We tell her that Cal wants to give her an award."

"What kind of award could she possibly win?" Courtney asked. "World's worst counselor?"

Everyone laughed.

"Don't forget," Stephanie reminded them, "Parker thinks she's got Cal wrapped around her little finger. She thinks Cal thinks she's the best counselor ever! We could tell her she's won an award for her excellent counseling," Stephanie said. "And that Cal wants to give her the award on the stage."

"Yes!" Michelle cheered. "She'll practically run up to the platform then!"

Shari suddenly cleared her throat. "Quiet, everyone! Parker's coming this way!"

Everyone began eating their lunch. Stephanie started reciting their schedule for the rest of the day.

"And then we have arts and crafts to put

the finishing touches on our dunk-tank booth," she said. "After that, it's free time, then dinner. Tonight is movie night, so—"

"Uh, Stephanie, can I talk to you for a second?" Parker interrupted.

"Sure." Stephanie nodded. "I'll be right back, guys," she said.

Parker pulled her aside. "So, exactly what happened between you and Cal last night at the campsite?" she asked.

Stephanie couldn't believe her nerve. *First she lies to me, then she laughs at me, then she wants me to tell her what happened like we're buddies or something!*

"Oh, nothing much," Stephanie lied. "He told me he thinks I'm doing a great job running the bunk. Isn't that great?"

An annoyed expression crossed Parker's face. "Oh, just wonderful!" she snapped.

"He also mentioned that I owed a lot of my success to working with you," Stephanie added.

Parker's face softened. She actually looked pleased. "He did?" she asked.

"Yup. Thanks *so much* for smoothing things over for me all those times," Stephanie went on. "You must have really said some great things. I guess you're responsible for him thinking I'm doing such a good job."

"Oh, that's nice," Parker said. She patted Stephanie's arm.

She is sooo fake, Stephanie thought. *I can't believe I didn't see through her right away.*

Parker cleared her throat. She checked her clipboard. "Uh, anyway, you're stuck with mess hall cleanup tonight."

Stephanie made a face. "Mess hall cleanup?" she asked.

"Each group is responsible for cleaning up after one meal during the week," Parker told her. "Tonight is your turn. Guess you'll have to miss the movie," she added. "Sorry."

"No, I'm sorry," Stephanie told her. "We already did mess hall cleanup. And there's no way my group is missing the movie."

"Oh, but, Stephanie. I know *Cal* will totally appreciate it," Parker insisted.

"I think my campers would appreciate going to the movie. You're going to have find someone else to clean up," Stephanie stated. "If you have a problem with that, we can always ask Cal his opinion."

Parker was fuming. She turned on her heel and stomped off.

Stephanie tried not to laugh as she hurried back to her table.

"What's going on?" Michelle asked.

"Parker just told me we had cleanup duty tonight. Can you believe it?" Stephanie smirked. "Cal probably gave *her* cleanup duty, and she was passing it down to me!"

Michelle and her friends exchanged worried looks. "We'll help," Michelle said. The other girls nodded.

Stephanie was touched. "Thanks. But you guys don't have to help," she said. "I told Parker we wouldn't do it."

"No way!" Mallory exclaimed.

"Yup." Stephanie felt proud of the way she handled it. "I bet she's totally furious!"

Michelle grinned. "Great. So let's get back to our plans for the carnival." She grabbed an Oreo cookie and dunked it into her milk.

Stephanie glanced at her watch. "Lunch is almost over," she said. "Let's meet after lights-out to plan the rest of Operation . . ." What was a good name for the plan to dunk Parker?

She glanced at Michelle, still dunking. "I know! Operation Oreo Cookie!"

The next days flew by. "I can hardly believe today is the camp carnival!" Stephanie checked the bunk. They had all gotten up early.

They had a big day ahead. They hurried to check out the dunking tank in the sports hut.

Stephanie marveled at how well the tank had turned out.

She was setting up the signs, when Cal walked into the hut.

"Hey, Stephanie!" he said with a smile. "I haven't seen you for a while."

Stephanie pulled her hair back into a ponytail, then slipped her baseball cap over her head. She had avoided Cal since the disaster at the campsite. She was still embarrassed when she thought about it.

"Hi, Cal!" she replied. "We wanted to get a head start on our booth."

Cal examined the dunk tank. "It came out great. This is awesome!"

"Thanks!"

"Listen, Stephanie," he began, "about the other night. I'm really sorry for what happened."

Stephanie shrugged. "It's okay," she said. "Thanks for covering for me in front of the others. I felt really silly."

"Well, I think I have an idea of how you could have been misled," Cal explained. "You told me Parker said I wanted to see you. I asked her a few questions about that, and she couldn't give me any good answers."

Stephanie started to say something, then decided to listen.

"Anyway," Cal continued. "I'm afraid I've known for a little while now that Parker likes me. Even though I think of her only as a friend. The point is, I think Parker may be jealous of you, and that's why she gave you the false information."

"But I don't understand," Stephanie said. "Why would Parker be jealous of me?"

"Because, uh," Cal mumbled. "Well, the thing is, I really *do* like you!"

Stephanie nearly fell over. "You do?"

Cal nodded. "You're a lot of fun, Stephanie," he said. "Maybe we can see each other sometime, when camp is over."

"Sure. That would be great," Stephanie told him.

Cal smiled. "Good. And I hope you come back again next year. You're really creative— and great with the kids."

Sure I am—now that I can be myself again! she thought.

Stephanie grinned. "Thanks. I'll think about it. But I'd better get back to work. There's still a lot to be done."

Michelle and the others ran up with the painted signs for the booth.

"These really came out great!" Stephanie said as she helped Michelle set them up.

"Definitely!" Michelle said. "I think they'll be lining up at the dunk tank from here back to San Francisco! Especially with Parker as the main dunk attraction."

"Are we all set with our plan?" Mallory asked.

"Operation Oreo Cookie is ready to go!" Stephanie replied. She had covered the large tank with a large sheet of material, so that it would look like a stage.

Then she gazed up at the platform and wooden bench above the dunk tank. It looked perfect. Parker's bench was positioned so she couldn't see the water. She would never suspect a thing.

"They already filled the tank with water," Michelle reported.

"This is going to be so cool!" Mallory exclaimed.

"Not *cool,* Mallory," Michelle joked. "*Cold!* This is going to be very *cold!*" All the Grape Jammers laughed.

Soon the area outside the sports hut began to fill with campers. They quickly pulled the dark curtains around the tank. Nobody could tell what it was. By lunchtime, the camp carnival was in full swing. Campers crowded the booths, playing ring toss, pitching softballs, or riding go-carts.

Stephanie and Michelle spent a half hour playing miniature golf at the Banana Floats' booth. Then it was finally time to get ready for Operation Oreo Cookie.

"Be sure to take lots of pictures," Stephanie told Allison. "You guys ready?" she asked. "And you all know what you're supposed to do?"

The girls nodded.

"Excellent! Let's do it!"

Chapter
16

I think I saw Parker talking to another senior counselor by the ring-toss booth," Stephanie said. "You guys go over there," she told Michelle and Jeannie. "Mallory and Courtney—you go and make sure Cal stays away."

"Come on, Jeannie," Michelle said.

Michelle and Jeannie headed over to the ring-toss booth and found Parker.

"Hi, Parker!" Michelle called out. "Hey . . . did Cal Mason find you?"

Parker froze. "What?" she asked. "Cal was looking for me? When? Where?"

Jeannie pretended she couldn't remember when she'd last seen Cal. "I don't know, maybe it was a half hour ago."

"What did he want?" Parker asked nervously.

Michelle's eyes widened. "It's about the award," she said.

Parker stared at her. "What award?" she asked.

Michelle and Jeannie exchanged glances.

"Are you kidding?" Michelle asked. "You mean you didn't hear?"

Parker shook her head. "No—hear what?"

Jeannie smiled proudly. "Oh, it's great news, actually," she said. "Cal said you were the best counselor in the whole camp this year. And he wants to give you an award for it."

Parker's face lit up. "Really?" she said. "He said that?"

Michelle nodded.

"That's why he was looking for you!" Jeannie added. "To give you the award."

"I'd better go find him," Parker said.

Michelle and Jeannie giggled as they watched Parker run across the hut.

Stephanie was waiting for her. "Parker! Over here!" she called.

"Stephanie? What's up? Cal is looking for me," Parker told her.

Stephanie nodded. "I know. He asked me to find you. Just follow me." Stephanie led Parker through the crowd, then around the back of the dunk tank.

Wait up there, on the stage," Stephanie told her. "Come on, it's dark, so I'll walk up with you."

Stephanie followed Parker up the steps.

"There's the bench! Have a seat right there, Parker."

Parker sat. Cal's voice came over the camp loudspeaker.

"And now, a very special event," Cal's voice boomed over a PA system. The announcement you've all been waiting for!"

"Get off the stage, Stephanie," Parker snapped. "This is *my* award!"

"No problem, Parker." Stephanie smiled to herself. "You're absolutely right. This is your award. You deserve it." She scurried down the steps.

"The highlight of the camp carnival this year," Cal announced, "the dunk tank!"

The curtains opened and Parker could suddenly see. Everyone looked up at Parker. "Wait a minute," Parker protested. "What's going on here? I'm supposed to be getting an award!"

Mallory whipped off the sheet covering the water tank.

Stephanie saw the panic on Parker's face as she realized what was going on.

"Here's your award, Parker!" she cried. "This is exactly what you deserve!"

Stephanie and the Grape Jammers each picked up a softball.

"Everyone ready?" she called. Together they counted. "One, two, *three!*"

On *three*, thirteen softballs went sailing through the air, headed straight for the dunk-tank target.

"Nooo!" Parker wailed.

A moment later she splashed down into the tank.

Stephanie, Michelle, and the Grape Jammers all cheered wildly.

Parker came up for air, sputtering. She was completely drenched.

"This is *not* funny!" she shouted from inside the tank. "I mean it, Stephanie! I'm going to report you for this!"

"For what? Having the longest line at the carnival?" Stephanie turned around and grinned. Every camper and CIT who was ever assigned to Parker's bunk was lined up behind her. Everyone wanted a turn to give Parker a dunking.

"Know what?" Michelle told her. "Going to camp together turned out to be a good idea after all!"

Stephanie and Michelle slapped a high-five. "Nice work, sister!" Stephanie told her with a grin.

"Right back at you, sister!" Michelle replied.

Stephanie grabbed Michelle and gave her a huge hug.

FULL HOUSE™
Michelle

#5: THE GHOST IN MY CLOSET 53573-0/$3.99
#6: BALLET SURPRISE 53574-9/$3.99
#7: MAJOR LEAGUE TROUBLE 53575-7/$3.99
#8: MY FOURTH-GRADE MESS 53576-5/$3.99
#9: BUNK 3, TEDDY, AND ME 56834-5/$3.99
#10: MY BEST FRIEND IS A MOVIE STAR!
(Super Edition) 56835-3/$3.99
#11: THE BIG TURKEY ESCAPE 56836-1/$3.99
#12: THE SUBSTITUTE TEACHER 00364-X/$3.99
#13: CALLING ALL PLANETS 00365-8/$3.99
#14: I'VE GOT A SECRET 00366-6/$3.99
#15: HOW TO BE COOL 00833-1/$3.99
#16: THE NOT-SO-GREAT OUTDOORS 00835-8/$3.99
#17: MY HO-HO-HORRIBLE CHRISTMAS 00836-6/$3.99
MY AWESOME HOLIDAY FRIENDSHIP BOOK
(An Activity Book) 00840-4/$3.99
FULL HOUSE MICHELLE OMNIBUS 02181-8/$6.99
#18: MY ALMOST PERFECT PLAN 00837-4/$3.99
#19: APRIL FOOLS 01729-2/$3.99
#20: MY LIFE IS A THREE-RING CIRCUS 01730-6/$3.99
#21: WELCOME TO MY ZOO 01731-4/$3.99
#22: THE PROBLEM WITH PEN PALS 01732-2/$3.99
#23: MERRY CHRISTMAS, WORLD! 02098-6/$3.99

A MINSTREL® BOOK
Published by Pocket Books

Simon & Schuster Mail Order Dept. BWB
200 Old Tappan Rd., Old Tappan, N.J. 07675

Please send me the books I have checked above. I am enclosing $_____ (please add $0.75 to cover the
postage and handling for each order. Please add appropriate sales tax). Send check or money order--no cash or C.O.D.'s please. Allow up to
six weeks for delivery. For purchase over $10.00 you may use VISA: card number, expiration date and customer signature must be included.

Name _____

Address _____

City _____ State/Zip _____

VISA Card # _____ Exp.Date _____

Signature _____

1033-28

FULL HOUSE Stephanie™

PHONE CALL FROM A FLAMINGO	88004-7/$3.99
THE BOY-OH-BOY NEXT DOOR	88121-3/$3.99
TWIN TROUBLES	88290-2/$3.99
HIP HOP TILL YOU DROP	88291-0/$3.99
HERE COMES THE BRAND NEW ME	89858-2/$3.99
THE SECRET'S OUT	89859-0/$3.99
DADDY'S NOT-SO-LITTLE GIRL	89860-4/$3.99
P.S. FRIENDS FOREVER	89861-2/$3.99
GETTING EVEN WITH THE FLAMINGOES	52273-6/$3.99
THE DUDE OF MY DREAMS	52274-4/$3.99
BACK-TO-SCHOOL COOL	52275-2/$3.99
PICTURE ME FAMOUS	52276-0/$3.99
TWO-FOR-ONE CHRISTMAS FUN	53546-3/$3.99
THE BIG FIX-UP MIX-UP	53547-1/$3.99
TEN WAYS TO WRECK A DATE	53548-X/$3.99
WISH UPON A VCR	53549-8/$3.99
DOUBLES OR NOTHING	56841-8/$3.99
SUGAR AND SPICE ADVICE	56842-6/$3.99
NEVER TRUST A FLAMINGO	56843-4/$3.99
THE TRUTH ABOUT BOYS	00361-5/$3.99
CRAZY ABOUT THE FUTURE	00362-3/$3.99
MY SECRET ADMIRER	00363-1/$3.99
BLUE RIBBON CHRISTMAS	00830-7/$3.99
THE STORY ON OLDER BOYS	00831-5/$3.99
MY THREE WEEKS AS A SPY	00832-3/$3.99
NO BUSINESS LIKE SHOW BUSINESS	01725-X/$3.99
MAIL-ORDER BROTHER	01726-8/$3.99
TO CHEAT OR NOT TO CHEAT	01727-6/$3.99
WINNING IS EVERYTHING	02008-6/$3.99

 Available from Minstrel® Books Published by Pocket Books

Simon & Schuster Mail Order Dept. BWB
200 Old Tappan Rd., Old Tappan, N.J. 07675

Please send me the books I have checked above. I am enclosing $_____ (please add $0.75 to cover the postage and handling for each order. Please add appropriate sales tax). Send check or money order--no cash or C.O.D.'s please. Allow up to six weeks for delivery. For purchase over $10.00 you may use VISA: card number, expiration date and customer signature must be included.

Name _____
Address _____
City _____ State/Zip _____
VISA Card # _____ Exp.Date _____
Signature _____

1229-25

It doesn't matter if you live around the corner...
or around the world...
If you are a fan of Mary-Kate and Ashley Olsen,
you should be a member of

MARY-KATE + ASHLEY'S FUN CLUB™

Here's what you get:
Our Funzine™
An autographed color photo
Two black & white individual photos
A full size color poster
An official **Fun Club**™ membership card
A **Fun Club**™ school folder
Two special **Fun Club**™ surprises
A holiday card
Fun Club™ collectibles catalog
Plus a **Fun Club**™ box to keep everything in

To join Mary-Kate + Ashley's Fun Club™, fill out the form
below and send it along with

U.S. Residents – $17.00
Canadian Residents – $22 U.S. Funds
International Residents – $27 U.S. Funds

MARY-KATE + ASHLEY'S FUN CLUB™
859 HOLLYWOOD WAY, SUITE 275
BURBANK, CA 91505

NAME:_____

ADDRESS:_____

_CITY:_____ STATE:_____ ZIP:_____

PHONE:(____) _____ BIRTHDATE:_____

TM & © 1996 Dualstar Entertainment Group, Inc.   1242